THAT CRAZY APRIL

Lila Perl

THAT CRAZY APRIL

THE SEABURY PRESS

NEW YORK

Copyright © 1974 by Lila Perl
Designed by Carol Basen
Printed in the United States of America

LIBRARY OF CONGRESS CATALOGING IN PUBLICATION DATA

Perl, Lila.
  That crazy April

  SUMMARY: A month of crazy and often upsetting events, including a hapless fashion show, causes an eleven-year-old to question her own outlook and role as a girl.
  [1. Family life—Fiction] I. Title.
PZ7.P432Th   [Fic]   73–14812
ISBN 0–8164–3117–5

For Joy
and her daughters,
Roby and Kyla,
with deep gratitude.
And with special thanks
to Sandy.

1

 The very first day of that crazy April is when this story really begins.

Davey and I were walking home to my house from the school bus stop.

"I can't get over it," Davey said. "April Fools' Day and not a single April-fool joke played in my class. Kids are too serious these days, Cress. I bet a lot of them didn't even know what day it was."

I agreed with Davey. Things had been quiet in my class, too. Oh, a few of the kids had sprinkled itching powder on Sheila Butterworth's seat and on Miss McCracken's desk chair. But Sheila had sat there without wriggling once the whole time, and Miss McCracken was in one of her walking-around-the-room moods and never sat down at all. I wouldn't be surprised if they'd sold those kids stale itching powder. So the joke was on them!

Anyhow, up to about half-past three in the afternoon on that April Fools' Day, my life was still pretty quiet and orderly.

We were living in this ultra modern glass-and-wood giant of a house sprawled across the top of a wooded hill in upper Westchester County, about thirty miles north of New York City. We had moved into the house a year earlier and I still thought it was much too big and show-offy for just my mother, my father, and me.

I had really liked the cramped, pointy-roofed, pistachio-colored, stucco house we'd been living in down in the lower part of the county. And I blathered a lot to my parents about how I didn't *want* to move out of the old house. Because when you're a shy, dumpy, ten-and-a-half year old girl, and an only child as well, you like to stay in one place so you can hold on to your friends.

But naturally my parents didn't listen to any of my objections or to my worries about how uncomfortable I'd be showing the house to any of my friends from the old neighborhood if they ever came to visit.

My father had just grinned and said, "It's the kind of place I've wanted to own all my life." And my mother didn't exactly disagree with him.

Well, as I said, that was a year ago, and I have to admit the part about making new friends turned out much better than I expected. In fact, it wasn't long before I'd made two favorite friends. One of them

 8

was Monique Patten and the other one was Davey —Davey Link.

Monique was a gorgeous silky-blonde model. My age! Imagine having a friend who's a real live fashion model. It's practically like being best friends with a movie star.

The main thing about Davey Link, I suppose, was that he was so terribly rich. His real name was David James Peter Link III and he came from what is known as an "old" family.

Davey lived in a house that some people said was a real eighteenth-century French chateau which had been brought over stone by stone from France. When I asked Davey about it, though, he just said he didn't know. So I never asked him again.

There was one other thing that I knew better than to ask Davey about. That was his mother. She was a real mystery. People called her the Missing Link. Terrible, isn't it?

Anyway, she'd run away or managed to disappear somehow when Davey was only five. Davey's father was a middle-aged naval officer who wasn't on active duty anymore. But he was on the boards of some big corporations and did a lot of traveling on business and government-type things. There was an elderly Scottish couple who ran the Link "chateau" and took care of Davey.

I liked Davey right off from the first time I saw him on the school bus. He was half-a-year younger than I was and half-a-head shorter, and kind of tousled and chubby, so maybe I thought of him as the little brother I wished I had and didn't have. Or maybe I just recognized him as another only child. Or maybe I just knew—being a cookie-baker—that Davey was a cookie-eater. And in this world you need somebody to take home with you at three o'clock for milk and cookies.

That's how come Davey and I were crunching our way up Carter Ridge Road, toward the foot of the steep gravel drive that leads to our house, on the first day of April.

"Tell you one thing," Davey remarked, glancing up at the big apple-green buds on an overhanging tree. "It won't be like this next year when I'm at the naval academy prep school. April Fools' Day will be *wild*. You can bet those navy guys will know how to do it."

Davey and his naval prep school talk! He looked so funny when he put on his naval cadet airs, and I had to laugh every time I thought of pudgy little Davey in a tight uniform.

But there was a serious side, too. Davey was going away to school in September and, even though I'd promised to send him cookies at least once a month, I knew it wouldn't be the same between us after he

 10

left. Lately, too, no matter what we were talking about, Davey always ended up saying how they did everything so much better at "old naval prep." And he hadn't even seen the place yet.

I suppose you couldn't blame Davey. He came from a long line of admirals.

By now Davey and I had nearly reached the mailbox at the bottom of our driveway. I stopped a moment to take off my shoe and shake out a pebble. Davey kept on walking. Just as I was straightening up, Davey called over his shoulder,

"Hey Cress, look here. Somebody's played an April-fool joke on you."

"Who? Where?"

Davey was standing in front of our mailbox. It was just an ordinary suburban letterbox nailed to a post. I couldn't figure out what anybody would find to do to it. I hurried over to see.

"Look at this," Davey said, pointing to two rows of big bold block letters stamped in red along the side of the mailbox. "New names."

I looked at the letters carefully. They were certainly big enough and clear enough. The first line read *Mary Dalton*. The second line read *Philip Richardson*.

"Oh that," I said. "That's nothing. Nothing at all. It's my mother's new idea."

I knew of course that my mother was planning to

change the names on the mailbox. But that morning, when I'd left for school, the small black letters—*Mr. and Mrs. Philip S. Richardson*—had still been on it.

Davey pushed out his lower lip and looked half-angry the way he always did when he didn't quite understand something.

"What new idea?"

"Well, it isn't all *that* new. The way my mother explains it, she's a person first and somebody's wife second. So why shouldn't she have her own name instead of somebody else's. That makes sense, doesn't it?"

"Is that your mother?" Davey planted a pudgy forefinger on the red M for Mary.

"Yes."

Davey put his head to one side. "Are you sure your parents didn't get divorced?"

I laughed. "Oh don't be stupid, Davey. They were still married when I saw them at breakfast."

"Well," Davey said uncertainly, "sometimes these things happen very suddenly." Poor Davey, maybe he was thinking of his own mother.

"No, no," I said. "Look. It's simple. Mary Dalton was my mother's name before she got married to my father. Now she's decided she wants to use it again, even if she is married. Don't you believe me?"

Davey shook his head stubbornly. "Women always take their husband's name when they get married.

 12

They even teach us that in school. Like if you write her a letter, you're supposed to address it . . ."—Davey turned to the mailbox—"Mrs. Philip Richardson."

"I know," I said, a little impatiently. "But all that's changing now. You'll see. It's all going to be different."

Davey narrowed his eyes. "How do you mean?"

"I mean . . . different." I jabbed a finger at the mailbox. "Like this!"

Davey let his books slam to the ground. "Cress Richardson, you're nuts!"

"Now look, Davey," I retorted, beginning to get a little steamed up at him, "don't get so huffy. You're not at naval prep yet."

He waved my remark away with his hand. "Well, why would you think it's a good idea for your mother to change back to her own name. Do you hate your father?"

"Of course I don't hate my father. I love my father. I love my mother, too. I love them equally and I don't think one is more important than the other. So why shouldn't my mother. . . ."

Davey was beginning to turn pink and steamy-looking. He pushed a hand through his already tousled hair and rolled his eyes up to the sky as though he was looking for sympathy or advice. Two wispy peaks of hair now stood straight up into the air.

13

"You know, Davey," I said in exasperation, "my mother said this is how a lot of men and boys would react. It's what my mother would call a 'typical male reaction.' She says. . . ."

"My mother says; my mother says," Davey mimicked. "My God, Cress, all I ever hear out of you lately is your mother this, your mother that. Over and over and over again."

"Oh really!" I snarled, breathing hard and talking right into his face. "And did it ever occur to you, Davey Link, that you might be just a little supersensitive on the subject of mothers?"

Davey's eyes opened wide in shock.

I realized right away that I'd said a pretty mean and stupid thing. But somehow I just couldn't stop myself.

"And since *you* don't like hearing the same thing over and over again," I ranted on, "let me tell you something about *that*. I am sick of hearing about your 'old naval prep' over and over again. For one thing, it isn't 'old,' as far as you're concerned. You hardly know anything about it. And you won't even be going there for another five months yet. *And* you might hate the place when you get there. Why, you might even flunk out!"

Davey and I just stood there for a moment, rooted to the spot and glaring at one another. Then, with one scoop of his arm he swept his books up off the

 14

ground, turned his back on me in a kind of military about-face, and marched off down the gravel driveway.

I enjoyed one solitary second of satisfaction. And then, the very next moment, I felt terrible!

On top of getting dangerously close to the subject of Davey's mother, I'd hit him in another place where it hurt because I knew he was worrying about going to the naval academy. With his father being an important naval reserve officer, doing really well at naval prep was going to be a big responsibility for Davey.

Furthermore, as to the subject of my own mother, I wasn't really all that sure how I felt. Since my mother had become interested in all these problems about women (which had a lot more to them than just getting to keep your own name after you got married), she had taken over one of the five bedrooms in the new house for a study. She had a desk full of paperwork and her own private telephone because she was on all sorts of committees and busy with all sorts of causes, and most of the time she was in there with the door shut.

In fact, my mother's new activities had been one of my biggest disappointments after we moved. When we had lived in the old house, she had had a job with a social welfare agency and she was away at work five days a week. Now that she *wasn't* work-

15

ing, she was sometimes away seven days a week, especially if she went to one of those conferences about the rights of women that were usually being held in places like Omaha or Dubuque or Chicago.

Weekends without your mother around can be particularly terrible. You and your father just sit and look at each other and try to make believe that it isn't Sunday outside and that everything is just dandy.

By this time, Davey was rapidly turning into a speck the size of a pinhead at the bottom of the driveway. And all I knew was that the cookie tin in the kitchen was full of delectable dream bars that I'd baked just for him the night before.

I cupped my hands around my mouth and yelled out as loud as I could, "Hey, *Day-veee!*"

Davey didn't turn. He just kept on marching.

"*DAVEY!!!*" I practically screamed. "I made those cookies for you. The kind you said you loved. The munchy ones with the chocolate chips in them. And the big chunks of walnuts."

I waited. No response. And then, very slowly, Davey turned.

He just turned and marched back up the driveway the same way he'd marched down, very stiffly and with his pudgy round shoulders really squared. I actually expected him to salute me when we came face-to-face again.

❀ 16

Instead he looked at me soberly and said, "You didn't put any coconut in them this time, did you? Because I hate coconut. It gets between my teeth and then it gets stuck in my throat and it makes me cough."

I nodded, feeling almost guilty because it was really so easy to get to Davey's heart through his stomach. "Nope, no coconut," I said. "I made them just the way you like them."

Davey was easy to get to but he was also pretty fussy and bossy. If he liked something he liked it and if he hated it he hated it. Like with the coconut. The way he gave orders, the girl who married him was going to have a rough time. She'd probably end up being Davey's slavey. Or else she'd run away and become another . . . Missing Link.

Well, as I said before, what could you expect from Davey? He came from a long line of admirals.

2

Nobody was home when Davey and I got to the house, and I had to unlock the door to let us in. I wasn't surprised. Lately my mother had been spending her afternoons at the new headquarters for women that had been set up to help women know their rights, like equal pay for equal work and things like that. I guess my mother had had the names on the mailbox changed that morning before she left.

Davey liked the dream bars all right. He never talked much when he was eating, just munched away on one cookie after another and gulped down his milk. He was beginning to get that glazed-over look that meant he was full when I heard a car crunching up the drive.

It gave me an uncomfortable feeling, somehow, thinking it was my mother and she'd walk in in a couple of seconds and find Davey sitting at the big round kitchen table, with me feeding his face. We'd been having a lot of arguments about that lately.

My mother didn't think that men should constantly be waited on by women. She said I fussed over Davey too much.

I jumped up from the table, pulled open the glass door, and dashed out onto the kitchen terrace. (Just about every room in that house had an outdoor balcony connected to it.) There was a little canary-yellow jalopy coming to a stop in front of the garage. It wasn't my mother at all. It was Xandra.

What a surprise!

"Hey Davey," I called into the kitchen. "My cousin Xandra's here."

When I looked around, Davey was just grunting and pouring some more milk into his glass. I was excited. Xandra here in the middle of the week and it wasn't even Easter time yet.

I waved from the balcony as Xandra hopped out of the car. She was wearing jeans and a white V-neck sweater with a striped shirt underneath.

"Xandra! Hi. What a surprise. What's up?"

She waved back.

"Great news, Cressie. Hey, how about coming down to open the door for me?"

I raced past Davey, scurried down the half-flight of stairs to the front hall and threw open the door. Xandra's cheeks were glowing.

"Oh Cressie. Yum, yum, yum," she said as she threw her arms around me. "Good to see you. Anybody home? Wow, have I got news for you!"

I loved Xandra. Her mother was my mother's older sister. But Xandra's family lived out West, in Arizona, and Xandra was going to college near us in the East, in Massachusetts. On long weekends and school holidays she usually came and stayed with us.

If Davey was the little brother I didn't have and wished I did, then Xandra was the big sister I'd always wanted. She was nineteen and just finishing her sophomore year at college. She was studying something complicated that involved a lot of chemistry and biology. Some day she was going to be doing research on the chemistry of body cells.

I sometimes thought that Xandra was everything I wanted to be. She was certainly everything I wanted to look like. She had a pale, heart-shaped face and lovely straight dark hair that always looked graceful and swinging and just right. It never stuck out in the wrong places like my crinkly-curly black hair which got bushy and tangled if I tried to grow it too long. And she didn't have big splotches of high red coloring on each cheek, like I had, which made me look like one of those silly painted rag dolls.

Xandra wasn't too short (like me) or too tall. She wasn't too chubby (like me) or too skinny. I thought she was just about perfect. And she was

 20

sweet, too. Kind and shining and sweet.

I guess all the noise of Xandra and me greeting each other had finally gotten Davey up off his chair. Because when we both looked up he was standing awkwardly at the top of the stairs.

"Hi Davey," Xandra called up cheerily. "And how are you?"

Davey tossed his head to get the hair out of his eyes. He straightened his shoulders, very naval-cadetlike. "I'm fine, thank you, ma'am."

Xandra bounded up the stairs with me puppy-dogging it behind her. "Did you bring a suitcase? How long are you staying?" I wanted to know.

Xandra shrugged. "I threw some stuff in the back of the car."

Davey was still standing there stiffly. He cleared his throat. "Say, Cress, I think I have to run along now. I'll just get my books and then I'll be going. I really liked those cookies. You'll be sure to send me that kind when I'm at . . . er, naval prep."

"You don't have to leave just because I'm here, Davey," Xandra said. "Stay a while."

Davey flung up one hand like a traffic cop. "Um, no thanks." He was blushing just slightly. "I have a feeling it's all going to be girl talk around here from now on. So long, Cress. See you on the bus tomorrow."

The front door banged shut behind Davey, and

Xandra gave me a mischievous smile. "You've been feeding him cookies again, haven't you?"

I pushed the half-empty cookie tin toward Xandra. "What's wrong with that? Have some."

Xandra sampled a cookie. "*Dee*-licious. Mind if I make myself a cup of tea?" Xandra got up to fill the teakettle. "And where is my Aunt M, pray tell?" Since my mother had never especially liked her name being Mary, she usually asked people to call her M. Not Em, but M.

"She's down at this new women's job center or whatever it's called. At least I think that's where she is. What's your news, Xandra? Tell me."

Xandra's eyes were dancing. I could tell it was good news.

"Well, I thought I'd tell everybody at once. Make it a real slam-bang announcement."

"Oh no, Xandra. That could be hours from now, till Mom and Dad both get home. Tell me now. Please."

Xandra dangled a tea bag over an empty cup, twirling it back and forth by the string. "I don't think so," she said slowly, teasingly. "Tell you what I will do, Cressie. I'll give you three guesses. If you guess what my news is, I'll tell you everything. All about it. If you don't guess, you have to wait until dinnertime."

 22

"Okay," I said. I liked to play games as much as Xandra did. And I knew she'd play fair.

"Just three guesses, now. Remember. And you get a yes or no answer. And no compound questions."

I nodded. My eyes were already closed. I was thinking hard. I could hear the teakettle whistling and then the clanking of Xandra's spoon stirring around inside the cup.

"Well," I said, opening my eyes, "you seem to be wildly happy about it so I'm sure it's good news. So here goes. My first guess."

Xandra just smiled down into her cup and didn't say anything.

"You won an award or a . . . a scholarship in chemistry or . . . biochemistry. Something like that."

Xandra stopped sipping her tea, propped her elbows on the table, and grinned from ear to ear.

I got it, I thought to myself. The very first time. Well, naturally, that had to be it. Xandra wasn't only beautiful; she had a brain, too. And she was going to have a brilliant career in science. Mom always said Xandra was going to be "one of the new breed of women," whatever that meant.

But just then Xandra's grin narrowed and her mouth formed a very small circle. A single word came out. "No."

"No?"

"No. And, missy dear, you only have two more questions."

"I know," I said, feeling sort of let down. I thought hard while Xandra sipped some more tea.

"Okay, I'm ready. This is the one I should have asked in the first place. I'm sure it's the right question. Question number two. You've got a new boyfriend. Right?"

Xandra's eyelids dropped and she moved her head slowly back and forth. "Wrong."

"You haven't got a new boyfriend?"

"That's right. You're wrong. I haven't got a new boyfriend. And you've got only one question left."

"One question," I breathed. Now I was really discouraged. "Well, I'm pretty sure this isn't it," I said doubtfully, "but I'll ask it anyway. You're going home for Easter."

Xandra shook her head. "Sorry, my sweet. That's not it either. You'll just have to wait." Xandra leaned forward across the table. "But believe me, it's a lot more exciting than any of those guesses of yours. And it's worth waiting for. There may even be fireworks."

"You mean to celebrate? Has it got something to do with the Fourth of July? Independence Day?"

"It could," Xandra murmured mysteriously, as she rose to take her cup to the sink and wash it.

 24

"My kind of independence day, anyway. It just could." Xandra turned. "By the way, should I be doing something about getting dinner around here?"

I shook my head. "Uh-uh. Don't bother. It's Dad's night to handle dinner. This whole week is his. See . . . on the chart."

Xandra nodded with a knowing smile and opened the cupboard door to look at the calendar taped to the inside. It was marked off with big red letters by the week. She had stayed with us enough times to know what the "system" was at our house.

Since my Mom had gotten so interested in the liberation of women, all the household chores had been divided up by means of a family conference.

For example, each person made his or her own bed, cleaned his or her own room, and did his or her own laundry in the washing machine. Since Mom and Dad shared the same room and the same bed, Mom had the job one week and Dad had it the next. Making my bed, cleaning my room, and doing my laundry were my responsibility.

The new house was a little too busting-out-all-over for me, after that pistachio-green hut we'd lived in since I was a baby, so I'd chosen the smallest of the five bedrooms for myself. I felt nice and cooped up in there. And besides, there wasn't as much cleaning to do. Anyhow, if I cleaned my room it got done; if not, it didn't. More or less, I cleaned it.

25

The system for meals was pretty much the same, except that each of us had our week to get the meals. That way, each person's turn came around every third week.

As Mom explained it, it was an old-fashioned and nonsensical idea that women were supposed to do the cooking and housecleaning while men were supposed to do the outdoor work like running the lawnmower and putting up the screens. It could all be switched around, or shared, or worked out any way that the particular family liked best.

In our house, anybody who ate food had to take a turn being responsible for buying the food, setting the table, and cooking and serving the meal. Breakfasts were easy enough for even me to manage, and each of us almost always had lunch out, at school or at work or wherever.

When it came to dinners, we had all sorts of choices. We could cook a whole family dinner from scratch, or we could serve frozen or canned meals, or we could bring in cooked food all ready to eat. I usually made "quick-fix" dinners out of things I picked off the supermarket shelves or found in the frozen-food department. Mom generally cooked meals from scratch. And when it was Dad's week "on," he might bring home a whole cooked dinner, such as a complete Chinese meal from egg rolls to fortune cookies, or he might even take Mom and me out to eat once or twice.

All of which reminded me, speaking of the "system," that my room was getting to the rat's nest stage because I hadn't made my bed in a week and also I didn't have any clean underwear left in my drawer. Xandra was standing out on the kitchen terrace off in some dream world of her own, so I flew into my room and down the basement steps with a bundle of bedclothes and other laundry.

Might as well clear the decks, I thought, for Xandra's big independence day news. And on April Fools' Day yet!

3

 Mom got home at about six. She's a medium-size person, with a medium-pretty face except that her nose is rather pointed and she always wears her hair, which is brown and a little streaked with gray, pulled back and pinned up in a bun.

One thing that keeps her from being too stern-looking is that she always smiles a lot. She was smiling now as she came in the front door with a big bulging dark-red envelope under her arm and a shoulder bag that was bursting open with even more notes and clippings and heaven-knows-what.

Xandra was setting the table that looked out onto the dining terrace, even though she wasn't supposed to. As I explained, it was the job of whoever provided the dinners that week to do the table setting and stack the dishwasher afterward. But Xandra was a lot like me. I wasn't supposed to feed Davey Link milk and cookies all the time, but I did.

Mom kissed Xandra and said how happy she was to see her. She didn't criticize Xandra for setting the table. I guess she figured guests had special privileges.

"Xandra has a surprise," I said, helping Xandra set out the napkins. "But she won't tell what it is until we're all here. When do you think Dad'll get home? If he isn't here soon I'll probably explode. It's something very exciting—absolutely revolutionary in fact. As important as the Fourth of July. I tried three guesses but I didn't even come close."

Mom and Xandra both smiled at me indulgently. How in the world can grown-ups be so patient?

Mom deposited her envelope on the floor, curled up in a corner of the sofa, took a cigarette from her bag and lit it. She isn't the sort of mother who comes home and puts on an apron or a housedress, or gets into a comfortable pair of shoes. I guess she's always comfortable just as she is. And anyhow, for two weeks out of three she's a dinner guest in her own home. You can't really argue with that.

Xandra kept prettying up the table while she chatted with Mom about nothing in particular. She had even cut some daffodils that were already blooming in a warm patch in the garden and arranged a bowl of them for a centerpiece. I didn't see how Xandra and Mom could stand the suspense. Even when Dad's car crunched into the drive, the two of them just went on murmuring to each other in soft, quiet voices.

29

Not me. I raced down to the driveway to meet the car. Sure enough Dad had brought the Chinese dinner tonight and in about four seconds flat I had it all upstairs and piled on the kitchen table. Dad just smiled in his crinkly-eyed good-natured way as I opened the brown-paper bags.

"How much did you *get?*" I squealed, peering into the paper containers one after another. Dad always bought three times more of everything than we needed.

"Well, as usual," he said, scratching his sideburn and grinning in that crooked way I loved, "I wasn't sure, so I took two from Column A, three from Column B, four from Column C—and, let me tell you, they had a lot of columns tonight . . ."

What can I tell you about my father except that he's a kind of an electronics genius and a hard worker, that I sometimes think he's a big show-off, and that I love him? All the time we were living in that pistachio-green house, Dad was inventing and developing gadgets that I couldn't possibly understand or explain, and buying up small electronics companies and selling them at a profit. It didn't happen overnight, and *I* certainly wasn't taking any notice, but my father was getting richer all the time. And pretty soon we were moving into the new house —the kind he'd always wanted.

shining. "The reason I won't miss Bill," she said softly but very distinctly, "is that I'm going with him."

There was the sound of a fork crashing onto a plate. Mom's. She picked up the fork quickly. "You're transferring to the University of Dublin?"

"Not exactly," Xandra replied, looking directly at Mom. "You see, Aunt M, Bill and I are getting married. We're planning to get married in June."

I jumped up from my chair and clapped my hands. "Whee! So that's the news." I rushed around the table to Xandra and hugged her. "Oh, I'm so happy for you!"

Dad jumped up. He kissed Xandra, too, and ran to get the champagne.

"Cress," Mom said, "sit down." Her voice was very cool and crisp. She turned to Xandra. "Congratulations," she said softly. The smile was back on her face. But her voice wasn't smiling. "Does getting married to Bill mean you're giving up your schooling and your career?"

"Well, yes it does," Xandra said. "For now, anyway. You see, I'll have to get a job over there. I don't know what yet. But something."

"Why?"

"Well, to support us both, Aunt M, and to help Bill get through medical school. We've figured it all out. We couldn't possibly afford to *both* go to school.

There just wouldn't be enough money to live on."

I leaned my elbows on the table resting my chin between my hands and gazed mooningly at Xandra. "Oh, that's wonderful, Xandra. You must really love Bill. You're making a real sacrifice for him."

"I'm not looking at it that way," Xandra said, glancing around at all of us. Dad was back at the table with a bucket of ice and the champagne. "I just feel I want to spend the rest of my life with him and that both our efforts should be poured into his career."

"Bravo," Dad cheered, and then added, "speaking strictly from a traditional male point of view, of course."

Mom gave him a half-serious, half-playful look, as if to say, "I'll speak to you later." To Xandra she said, "But what about *your* career?"

Xandra shrugged. "I probably can't have it if I go with Bill. And I can't let him go without me. He'll be away for years. I'd lose him, don't you see?"

"He's that important to you?"

"Yes."

Mom tapped her fingernail against the rim of the glass as she spoke. "I don't want to sound like the voice of doom. But what if the marriage doesn't last? So many don't these days. Bill would have his medical degree, the one you helped him get. But all you'd have would be two years of uncompleted college work and four years of working in a shop or an office in Dublin."

Xandra shook her head. "It's no use, Aunt M. Bill and I have talked about this. There's no other way to do it. Anyhow, I'm not so sure biochem is really the field for me. I'm already having trouble with some of the science courses."

"Are you sure you aren't just talking defeatism to yourself? You know, to make leaving college seem unimportant? Anyhow, there are all sorts of other career courses you could switch to if you decided against science."

Xandra tossed her hair. "I'm sorry you can't be happy for me. I wanted to tell you and Uncle Phil and Cress first because you've been closer to me than my own family since I've been here in the East. I guess I knew you wouldn't approve of my giving up on a career for marriage. But I wouldn't be true to myself if I *didn't* do what I'm doing. That's why I told Cress this was going to be *my* declaration of independence."

I wanted to tell her how right *I* thought she was to marry Bill even if it did mean dropping out of college. Maybe she could go back later on, after Bill became a doctor. But Mom was speaking.

"Xandra, don't get me wrong. I respect your right to make this decision, even though I think you're confused. Just one question. Suppose *you* were the one who had gotten into medical school. Would Bill give up college to take an ordinary unskilled job so he could support you and make a home for you while you studied for a medical degree for four or five years?"

Xandra looked stunned. "I honestly don't think so."

"Even if you were going to be a very good doctor? Even if you were going to be a much better doctor than Bill will ever be?"

"But how could we know that?"

Mom sighed. "I guess we never will know that, Xandra. Not as long as women go on believing they are second-class people and keep on stepping aside to give men nearly all the chances to be doctors, engineers, presidents. . . ."

I kept wanting to say something. But what? Mom was getting me awfully confused. The idea of a man working, keeping house, cooking and cleaning and maybe even taking care of children while his wife went to medical school to become a doctor! It sounded crazy. Could it really work both ways?

Xandra grinned shyly. "Well, I *know* I wouldn't be any good as a doctor."

"But you're sure Bill will," Mom teased. "Now that's blind faith for you."

"Enough theorizing," Dad said. "Let's celebrate!"

There was a loud pop. I jumped, and Dad poured the champagne.

"To Xandra and Bill," Dad toasted.

"To Xandra and Bill," I said, carefully tipping the edge of the glass to my lips. To me, champagne was just sour ginger ale.

"Right," Mom echoed. "To Xandra and Bill." She tipped her glass sharply and took a long, strong swallow. But I could tell her heart wasn't in it.

I felt for Xandra's hand under the table and squeezed it hard. I was really angry at the way Mom had spoken to her. And somehow I wanted Xandra to know it and to know that I didn't feel that way about it at all. I felt exactly the opposite.

Xandra looked at me quickly and I thought I saw a tear shining in the corner of her eye. Or maybe it was perspiration. Or just a trick of the light.

Early the next morning, Xandra left.

I heard her tiptoeing past my door and jumped out of bed. I hadn't been asleep for quite a while, even though it was only just beginning to get light.

"Xandra!" I whispered. "You're going back to school?"

"Yes. I have a nine o'clock class and I can make it if I leave now."

"Xandra, please don't go without telling me. Who's right? You or Mom? I've got to know."

Xandra looked around her, shivering. She hadn't even brought a jacket with her.

"I can't tell you that," she hissed uncomfortably. " 'Right.' 'Wrong.' That's crazy."

"Then why did you come down here to tell us? You knew she wouldn't like the idea. She's always talking about women becoming astronauts, presidents, steamfitters, racedrivers . . . anything they choose."

"Okay. I choose to be Bill's wife. What's wrong with that?"

"Mom says that's not free choice, really. A wife is something every girl is expected to be some day. She's got to be her own person as well. A man never settles for being just a husband."

"Look, I can only speak for myself. I want to marry Bill. That's the real me. But you, Cress," Xandra said, bending and cupping my face between her hands, "you better try to make up your own mind about these things. And most important of all, find out who you are."

"Who I am?"

"Uh-huh."

I rubbed my eyes. It was too early in the morning and I could tell Xandra was anxious to leave. "Will I see you again? You and Bill?"

"Of course, silly. We'll come down in a couple of weeks."

I kissed her. I had a sinking feeling they wouldn't. I wanted to ask if I could at least come to the wedding, even if Mom and Dad didn't. But she was gone already. A moment later I could hear her starting up the jalopy, as quietly as possible.

Suddenly I knew that I, too, wanted to be out of the house before Mom got up. I could just see that sharp nose and that smiling mouth. It was infuriating the way she was always so sure about things. So I dressed, took a quick breakfast of milk and graham crackers, got my books together, and decided

41

to walk down the hill to Monique's house and catch the school bus from there.

My friend, Monique Patten, lived in a Southern-style mansion with a big front portico that had eight tall white pillars. The house was named *Tara* after the plantation house in that old movie, *Gone With the Wind*. Actually, Monique's house had been built only about ten years ago and Monique's mother came from Cincinnati, not Georgia or Tennessee or Mississippi. But it was an impressive-looking house just the same.

Monique came to the door looking just like a Southern belle on a summer's morning down South. Her long silvery-blonde hair was tied with a blue satin ribbon and she wore a long white dressing gown sprigged with bits of baby-blue embroidery and trimmed with narrow ruffled lace edging. She was chewing on a piece of buttered toast. The butter was dripping off onto her long slender fingers.

Monique didn't seem a bit surprised to see me there so early. I usually called for her a couple of times a week on nice mornings. "Oh," she said, matter-of-factly. "You heard."

I looked at her, baffled.

"No. What happened?"

"You didn't hear? Then how come you came to

 42

call for me today? And so early? I'm still eating breakfast. Come on in."

Monique shut the front door behind me and I followed her into the breakfast room. Her mother, who had been a big-name fashion model (before she married Monique's father), and who still did things like TV commercials and announcing at fashion shows, was just getting up from the table.

Mrs. Patten was so gorgeous and glittery and untouchable-looking that I always felt a little nervous in her presence, even though she was very friendly and never seemed to give herself any airs on purpose. Maybe the thing that really frightened me was her height. She was nearly six feet tall.

"Well, good morning, Cress," she said, smiling pleasantly. "Aren't you the early bird." A moment later all six feet of her were towering above me. "I'm awfully sorry. I've just *got* to dash."

Monique sat down at the table which had a glass top and curlicued white wrought-iron legs. She nodded for me to sit down, too. I plunked into one of the matching white wrought-iron chairs. "She's making an early plane to Palm Beach. You know, in Florida. She's coordinating some big fashion show for charity at one of the country clubs down there."

"Ooh, exciting."

Monique waved a limp wrist at me with her left hand, while she picked up her cup of cocoa with the other one. "She does things like that all the time."

"I know," I said faintly. I wondered why I didn't tell Monique and the other kids at school every time my mother caught an early-morning plane to some faraway city where a women's rights conference or political meeting was being held. Maybe I never told about those things because I was afraid they wouldn't seem very glamorous or exciting to people like Monique.

"So what's this big thing that happened that I didn't hear about?"

Monique put down her cup and took another triangle of buttered toast. "You mean to tell me that Dorothea Langley didn't phone you about it? Oh, she's impossible!"

"About what?" Dorothea was a friend of Monique's who always went around looking like a bad imitation of her. I didn't care for her too much.

Monique leaned forward. "Well, you're going to *love* this, Cress. It's a great chance for you. And you're just so perfect for the part."

"What do you mean 'part'?"

"Well, keep sitting down. Because here goes. I've got a spot for you in the Blair & Harper bridal fashion show!"

"In the bridal show? Me?"

Monique nodded and bit off a tiny corner of toast, looking very pleased with herself. Blair & Harper was one of the most elegant department stores in the East. Every year in April they gave a big bridal show in their main suburban store in Westchester. People came from all over to see it, so they scheduled several 'performances.' It showed what everybody in the bridal party should wear during the big June-to-September wedding season, all the way from the bride's grandmother to the tiniest toddling flower girl. For two years, now, Monique had been the main flower girl.

"I just don't believe it. Oh Monique, you're a terrific friend to think of me. But what would I be in the show?"

Monique pushed away her empty cup and leaned back. She was always very poised, never excited. I guess that was part of being a good fashion model. I wished I could control myself like that instead of usually acting and feeling like an excited puppy dog, the way I was now.

"You'd be a graduated flower girl."

"A *what* flower girl?"

"Graduated. You see, they're having eight flower girls this year. After me, of course—I'm the lead flower girl, as usual. Well, they're going to loop each line of four girls together with garlands of white camellias and green smilax accented with tiny apricot-yellow rosebuds. Now the girls have to be graduated in size, starting with the tallest pair first and

45

then on down to the peewees. That's where you'd fit in. See, I remembered that when we were measured in gym class a couple of weeks ago you were only four feet two. And that's just the height they're looking for. You'd be ideal because they don't want to have kids in the show who are too young."

"Gee," I said, still feeling pleased, "sometimes it pays to be short." I was going to add "and dumpy" but I left it out. Why call anybody's attention to that? And Monique hadn't said anything about the flower girls having to be thin.

"Dorothea could just kill you, I suppose," Monique commented. "She missed out because she's two inches too tall, and they have all the taller flower girls picked already. Maybe that's why she didn't phone you. I did honestly tell her to when they sent her home last night, and she said she would. I didn't get home from rehearsal myself until after ten."

It turned out that there was another rehearsal scheduled for that evening from six to eight P.M., and that the Pattens' maid, Geraldine, who came from the West Indies, would drive us to the Blair & Harper store in the Upper Westchester Shoppers' Mall.

Monique started up the winding front staircase to get dressed for school. "The new copy of *Chic* just came," she called back over the curving mahogany

 46

bannister. "It's on the hall table next to the flowers. Why don't you look through it while you're waiting? It's full of June bridal stuff."

I sat down on the cane-backed love-seat in the polished entry hall and flipped through the glossy pages of *Chic*. It was full of silverware patterns and crystal and china, as well as lacy bridal veils and creamy wedding gowns, and skimpy beach clothes for 'that honeymoon in the sun', and skimpy long dresses for 'cocktails by the pool', and even skimpier 'sleepwear'—although it was sometimes hard to tell which was which.

Chic called itself 'the magazine of fashion in your life'. Everyone in its pages was beautiful and slim, and tall, and young, and looked radiantly happy. I thought of Xandra and suddenly I felt sad. Xandra probably wouldn't have any of these beautiful things. She would be poor for quite a while, at least until Bill finished medical school and started to practice.

Monique came clattering down the stairs, carrying her books and a hatbox-shaped case made out of what looked like tapestry. "I nearly forgot. I've got twirling practice today after school." She tapped the case, which was new, and I realized her majorette's costume was in it. Monique was fantastic at baton-twirling. Sometimes I stayed after school to watch her and the other cheerleaders practice in their high

47

white boots, short, short satin skirts, and tall fancy hats.

"You really ought to get into twirling," Monique said, as we hurried for the bus. "You're not too short for that."

"I know," I said. "But I just think I'd be rotten at it. I'm sure I'd drop the stick. Anyway, I was thinking I'd join that new after-school metal-sculpture club that's starting next week."

Monique looked sideways at me and smiled slyly. "Oh, to meet boys, huh?"

"No, to do metal-sculpture. There's something I've been wanting to make—an owl out of different-shaped pieces of metal all clustered together. I saw one like that in a museum and it was beautiful. I even made a sketch of it that I keep in my room. I'd like to have a real one, of metal that is."

"Metal shop's filthy," Monique said, looking straight ahead at the approaching bus. "Only boys are in it because it's dangerous work cutting metal with power tools and welding with torches and all that. I'm not even sure they're letting girls into the club."

"It's no more dirty or dangerous than lots of other kinds of work women do," I argued.

We were on the bus by that time, saying hi to the kids we knew and having to separate to find places to sit. I looked around for Davey, wanting to tell him about my being a flower-girl in the Blair & Harper bridal show. I expected him to be pretty impressed. Even though I didn't look like Monique, it was nice to know that I could be a fashion model too.

But I couldn't see Davey's squashed-together face or rumpled brown hair anywhere. The bus started with a lurch and I sank into the nearest seat. Someone tugged at my arm. It was Roger Hollister in a seat directly across the aisle. "Looking for Davey?" he said. "I'm supposed to tell you he isn't coming to school today. He's sick."

I stared at Roger in surprise. He was a tall boy with the beginnings of a few dark moustache hairs on his upper lip. He lived about a half-mile from Davey's house. Sometimes he and Davey went fishing together at Grover's Lake. They rode their bikes there and were always talking about building a secret clubhouse in a thick clump of bushes near the shore.

"What's wrong with him?"

Roger had a dark look in his eyes. "He says he thinks it was those cookies you baked for him. He was throwing up all night. And he couldn't eat any breakfast."

"Really?" I was shocked.

Roger nodded solemnly. "Hey, what did you put in those cookies anyway?"

"Why nothing. Nothing bad. Lots of chocolate chips. Twice the amount the recipe says. Because he likes them so much. I was only trying to please him."

Roger looked up at the ceiling of the lurching bus and whistled. *"Please* him? You probably poisoned him. Don't you even know how to make cookies? What could be simpler?"

I glared at Roger. "Oh, shut up. Of course I know how to make cookies. He's probably got a stomach virus. Or indigestion from stuffing one cookie after another into his mouth. And gulping down I don't know how many glasses of milk. He probably went home and ate a whole big dinner besides. If he's sick, it's his fault and not mine."

Roger listened with a frozen smile on his face. Then he turned to the boy on the seat next to him and started whispering and giggling. I turned away in disgust. I never could understand what Davey saw in Roger Hollister. I think he was just flattered that Roger paid attention to him because he was older than Davey.

It was a big relief to get off the bus in the school driveway and catch up with Monique. She was murmuring something to herself over and over again, as though she was trying to memorize it.

"Do you have a test today, or what?"

Monique stopped a moment. "Me? Oh, no. It's the new cheer we have to learn. I want to get it perfect."

 50

"Is it hard? How does it go?"

Monique closed her eyes. "Let me see if I can do it. I'm thinking about the movements, too, you understand." Very slowly, she began,

> "Firecracker, firecracker
> Boom, boom, boom. . . .
> The boys have the muscles,
> The coach has the brains,
> The girls have the sexy legs
> To win all the games!"

Monique opened her eyes. "Wow, I think I've got it."

"Let's see if I can do it," I said. I closed my eyes like Monique and without any trouble I repeated the cheer.

Monique clutched my arm.

"You're good! You're very, very good. I told you, Cress, you *should* go out for twirling. You could do it."

I shook my head. "No Monique, I really don't think I could."

"But why, you silly thing, why not?"

"Well," I said, haltingly, "for one thing . . . well, for one thing I haven't got sexy legs."

Monique's eyes swept downward across my legs.

"Oh," she said, batting her lashes a couple of times and looking straight at me, "oh, good point. I never thought of that."

51

5

Wouldn't you know it? When I went to the metal-shop room during free period to put my name down for the after-school sculpture club, there was Roger Hollister helping Mr. Grinnell, the shop teacher.

Roger looked up with a surprised, slightly mocking grin when I came in the door. But he didn't say a word. Mr. Grinnell was friendly-looking in a grandfatherly way. He was portly, wore thick-rimmed glasses, and a gray wool vest buttoned across his broad belly.

"Yes, miss, what can I do for you?" he inquired as I approached the tool bench where he was working.

I told him about how I'd noticed the poster announcing the new after-school club only the day before. And even as I was explaining that I wanted to put my name down for it, I knew that the reason I wanted to make the metal owl so badly was that I wanted to give it to Xandra for a wedding present.

 52

Xandra had a little collection of bird and animal figures that she had bought at gift desks in museums and places like that. The owl I had in my mind would be perfect for Xandra. Perfect.

Mr. Grinnell wriggled his forehead so that his glasses dropped with a soft thud onto the lower part of his nose. He looked at me over the tops and said, "Have you ever done any work with metal before, young lady?"

"Oh, yes. At camp. In the summer. I made a beaten copper ashtray and a copper-and-bronze pendant. They're at home but I can bring them in if you want me to."

Mr. Grinnell looked doubtful.

"Have you ever done any welding?"

"No." I hesitated. "But I soldered. The pendant I mentioned—it has a couple of parts soldered onto the main piece, the base, as part of the design."

Mr. Grinnell scratched behind his ear, tilting his glasses to one side. Roger, who was tinkering over at a closet in the corner of the room, turned around very slowly and just looked.

"Ever work with power tools?" Mr. Grinnell asked.

I thought hard for a moment. "Yes," I said. "I have."

"What sort of tools?"

"Well . . . an electric knife, for one."

Mr. Grinnell pushed out his lower lip and looked at me sternly. Did he think I was trying to be funny?

"It's a power tool," I said defensively. "And a dangerous one, too. You can do plenty of damage with it if you don't know how to use it properly. But I'm so good at it I do practically all the family carving."

Mr. Grinnell didn't seem to be convinced.

"Well, it isn't really that different from a metal-cutting power tool, is it?" I urged.

Mr. Grinnell went over to his desk, took a blank pad of ruled yellow paper out of the drawer and pushed it toward me. "Put down your name here, and your class and room number. I'll have to see how many names are on the list already. I can't take more than fifteen in the club. Twelve really ought to be the maximum. There might be too many names down already."

"But there aren't any other names down here," I said. "There's just mine."

"I know, I know," he said with a trace of irritability. "I've got the list in my drawer somewhere. I'll have to check it."

"When will I know? You see, I want to make this owl for my cousin, to give her as a wedding present. She's getting married in June and the timing would be just right if I got into the club now. I have a sketch so I know exactly how I want it to look. I could bring it in to show you. . . ."

"Fine. I'll let you know if there's room."

"The club starts next week. Right?"

"That's right. Friday afternoons at 3:15, for ten sessions." The desk drawer slammed shut with the ruled yellow pad inside and Mr. Grinnell started back toward the tool bench where Roger was standing and smiling at me openly now. But I couldn't really say it was a friendly smile.

I didn't expect my mother to be home after school. And she wasn't. But Dad was there, hunched over the desk in his study with a big sheaf of papers in front of him. There was a delicious smell coming from the kitchen—a pie in the oven, I decided, apple or cherry.

It turned out to be a frozen apple pie, the kind that comes all ready to bake. Dad sometimes did this when it was his week "on" according to the meal schedule. He came home early with some of his office work so he could pop a whole frozen dinner in the oven. He found all sorts of interesting things in the frozen-food section of the supermarket—crabmeat au gratin, chicken a la king, macaroni and cheese. And when he began to run out of ideas toward the end of the week, he was very good at whipping up

55

Western omelets and salads and things like that.

"Have I got news for you!" I breathed, leaning straight across his desk and messing up his papers.

Dad clapped his hands together in a big noisy smack. "Hold on. Don't tell me. Let me guess. Let's see now . . . ah . . . er . . . I know. You're marrying Davey Link and going away to naval-cadet school with him."

I flopped down into a chair in the corner of the study. "Very funny. Poor Xandra. Did you know she left here before seven this morning? I think her feelings were hurt. She wanted us all to be happy for her and wish her luck."

Dad looked serious. "I know. Well, we did."

"Not *all* of us," I said pointedly. "Not really."

Dad put some papers to one side. "Well, never mind about that now. What's your big news?"

I began to tell him about the Blair & Harper bridal show, thinking how strange it was everything seemed to have to do with weddings all of a sudden. "I'll even get paid," I told him proudly. "Even for the rehearsal time, Monique says. Say, maybe I could be a model some day. A short model. If I don't grow any taller, that is. Well, they must need *some* short models to model clothes for short ladies. Or does everybody have to be tall? And thin?" I thought about the fashion models in *Chic* and realized that they probably did.

 56

Dad got up from his desk and put a nice warm broad hand on the back of my neck. "Come on, model, into the kitchen and I'll cook you a ham-and-cheese omelet. If you have to be at Monique's house by 5:30, you haven't much time and you're going to miss dinner altogether."

"Don't be silly," I said, trying to twist my neck around and look up at him as he piloted me out of the study. "I can cook my own omelet."

"Uh-uh. It's my night on. So I'm the cook. Do you want your mother to have a fit?"

Dad was already getting the eggs and other things out of the refrigerator. I sat down leaning my elbows on the big round wooden kitchen table.

"Don't you ever mind it?"

Dad cracked an egg. "Mind what?"

"Oh, you know . . . cooking, food shopping, housecleaning, laundry. Taking care of me, even."

"Sure I mind. About as much as your mother minds. Most of that stuff's no particular fun. Except the part about taking care of you, of course. And I missed the best part of that."

"How?"

"Well, until you were born your Mom worked. Then she quit and stayed home and took care of you until you were old enough to go to nursery school. Then she went back to work. After a while, she got pretty unhappy about having two full-time jobs. Until we sat down one day and talked about it, and worked things out pretty much the way they are now."

"But she isn't really working now. I mean, she's away from home but she isn't earning any money at it."

Dad waved an egg beater at me.

"Uh-uh. That's not how it's measured. It isn't the size of the paycheck or even the lack of one that matters. Work is work. Take most housewives. They work a lot more than eight hours a day. But they don't get any salary at the end of the week."

I nodded. "That's true, I suppose."

"Anyhow, it isn't who does the dishes that counts. It's cooperating so that no one is forced to do a chore simply because of his or her sex. Everyone should have the chance to be a . . . . a person."

"I suppose. . . . Still, I wish Mom had been nicer to Xandra last night."

"She was okay." Dad was beating the eggs so hard, sweat stood out on his forehead. "She was just disappointed. She thinks Xandra has a very good mind and isn't going to get a chance to use it because she has such a pretty face."

I thought about that a moment. Probably the same thing would happen to Monique. Definitely it would. But it wouldn't matter so much. Monique hated school already and only just got by in class.

 58

Or would Monique be doing better in her subjects if she didn't have her face and figure to fall back on? That is—would she be more like me?

"Maybe Bill is different," I said. "Maybe he's more understanding—like you—and he'll see to it that Xandra gets a chance to develop into something more than just Bill's wife. It's a possibility, isn't it?"

Dad poured the eggs into the sizzling butter in the frying pan. "You know what?" he said. "You worry too much."

A few minutes later he flipped a meltingly beautiful ham-and-cheese omelet onto my plate.

"Here, eat up and stop fretting. They don't want gray-haired flower girls in the Blair & Harper bridal show. Salad or sliced tomatoes with your egg?"

"And that's another thing. Oh, tomatoes, please. What's Mom going to say about this modeling? I'm pretty sure she'll be against that, too."

"Let's wait and see how *you* like it first."

"Oh, I'll like it all right. Don't worry about that." I crammed a large forkful of egg into my mouth. "This omelet's delicious. You're the greatest cook."

Dad beamed. I could tell he was pleased. "Just you remember, the greatest cooks in history have been male chefs."

"Then why do most men try their best to stay out of the kitchen? They might have hidden talents. Like you."

"Want to know the real reason? I'll tell you."
Dad happened to be washing the omelet pan just
then. "It's scrubbing the pots. What are the two
jobs that men look down upon the most? Why, being
a dishwasher in a restaurant and doing K.P. in the
army."

"Speaking of the army reminds me of the navy. I
have to phone Davey Link as soon as I finish eating."

To my surprise and relief, Davey answered the
phone himself. He sounded fine. He even seemed to
be munching on something.

"I thought you were sick."

"I'm not."

"But this morning. I saw Roger on the bus and
he said . . ."

"Oh, this morning. Oh, yeah. When old Rodge
stopped by I was feeling like the devil."

"You even told him you got sick from eating my
cookies."

"Did I? Sorry about that, Cress. I was feeling so
rotten I might have said anything." He was definitely
munching on something.

"Well, you should be more careful and not blame
other people for your pigginess. Roger got me very
angry on the bus."

Davey was silent. After a while he murmured,

 60

"Sorry. Honest, I'm awfully sorry, Cress. What can I tell you?"

I sniffed.

"Uh, anything happen at school today, Cress? Anything new?" I could tell he was feeling apologetic.

"Well, not at school exactly. But. . . ." And I told him about being a flower-girl in the Blair & Harper bridal show.

"Wow, Cress. I've got to hand it to you."

"Thanks," I said, trying to think of what I'd really done so far to deserve praise for getting into the show. Even being four feet two wasn't anything I could take credit for.

Davey's voice grew somber. "I guess that means you'll be too busy to do anything else this weekend, eh, Cress?"

"Why?" I asked curiously.

"Oh, it's not all that important, I guess."

"Come on, Davey, what is it?"

"Well, it's just that I was going to invite you to the lake. Fishing."

"When?"

"Saturday. Rodge and some of the guys are about ready to start building the clubhouse. You know, the one I told you about. Thought we'd ride out there for the day and start making plans. Also do a little fishing. The guys always say they don't want any girls along because this clubhouse is supposed to be a secret set-up. But I'll insist. I'll tell them if there's one girl we can trust it's Cress."

"That's nice of you, Davey." I just ached with wanting to say yes I could definitely come. I'd have to pray there wouldn't be a rehearsal. And that it wouldn't rain either.

"But if you're going to be tied up with this fashion show thing. . . ."

"Oh, no. I mean, not necessarily. I'll find out about Saturday and tell you for sure as soon as I can. Oh, and if I can come I'll fix a picnic lunch. How's that?"

"Now that would be terrific. Uh, did I ever tell you the kind of pickles I like best with corned beef sandwiches?"

"No, but you could tell me tomorrow, Davey. I'll be late for Monique's if I don't leave real soon."

"Right you are. See you tomorrow."

I ran to my room to get ready. There wasn't really anything I could do with my splotchy red cheeks or my impossible crinkly hair, or even my clothes. Monique had said that I shouldn't worry too much about my appearance because the people at Blair & Harper would "do" me.

I was nervous but I was happy. Suddenly there seemed to be so many exciting things happening in my life, so many things to look forward to—the

 62

bridal fashion show, the metal-sculpture club, going fishing at Grover's Lake with Davey and his crowd. It was only the second day of April and already it seemed as if everything was changing.

There was only one thing that didn't feel right somehow. It didn't even become clear to me until I had kissed Dad goodby and was hurrying down Carter Ridge Road toward Monique's house. But there it was. There was something wrong between my mother and me.

Had it only started last night at the dinner table with Xandra? Or had it been brewing for a long time? I realized that I felt more uneasy and confused every time I thought of Mom, that it would be hard to talk to her now, and that she wasn't around much to talk to anyway because she was so busy "liberating" women all over the country.

"Who's right?" I'd asked Xandra that morning. Well, in only one day I had come a lot closer to the answer. Xandra was too polite, too loyal to say it. But my mother just had to be wrong.

6

 On Thursday nights the Blair & Harper store stayed open until nine o'clock. It was jammed with shoppers this close to Easter. But after Geraldine (who said she "might as well become a full-time taxi driver") dropped us off at one of the main entrances, Monique knew just where to go. I followed closely as she threaded her way through the crowds, not hesitating to poke a slender elbow into someone's unsuspecting back when necessary.

Pretty soon we were in the Bridal Salon on the second floor. It was quiet there, with lush carpets and crystal chandeliers, and walls of mirrors. Monique led the way into the fitting rooms that were next to the custom workrooms.

"Stay here," she commanded, leaving me in the corridor outside a row of curtained fitting rooms. "No, wait a minute." She peeked into one of the curtained rooms. "This one's empty. Stay in here. I'll tell Cheryl you're in. . . ." she stepped back to read the number on the outside, "42." Cheryl Hawkins was the fashion consultant for the bridal show. She also happened to be a good friend of Monique's mother.

It was a big room for a fitting room, not the usual cubicle. Again, mirrors all around. I sat down on one of the pink plastic stools. My image stared back at me. I could see the front, sides, and back, all by looking straight ahead.

I looked completely out of place in there. A short fat creature in crumpled dungarees, and my hair sticking out in all directions because it was a damp evening. This was a room for tall slender young brides in long lovely dresses, turning slowly and admiringly before the mirrors while their mothers and aunts and all the fitters and salesladies oohed and aahed. I dropped my chin between my hands and wondered how much longer I would have to wait.

I could hear the buzz of conversation from unseen people in some of the other dressing rooms. Suddenly, almost next to my right ear, there was a rustling sound and immediately after that a piercing scream followed by the words, "It's *eggshell!*"

"Not at all, my dear," a soothing voice said. "It's cream. It's exactly what you ordered."

"Don't tell *me*," the young angry voice retorted. "It's eggshell. This is not the fabric we ordered for this gown."

"Angelica, please," someone said in a deep-pitched maternal voice, "don't get so hysterical. I'm warning you, one of us isn't going to live through this wedding. It looks like cream to me. Maybe it's the lights. I'm sure Blair & Harper wouldn't do such a thing."

"Oh, no?" said the angry bride-to-be sarcastically. "Well, I say it's eggshell and I won't be married in it."

"Sssh. People can hear you," said the deep-voiced mother. "There are other dressing rooms all around us."

"Try it on," said the soothing voice. "You can't tell a thing until it's on."

Angelica's high-pitched vinegary voice grew muffled. Probably they had the wedding gown, eggshell or cream, wrapped around her head by now. At that moment someone clutched frantically at the curtains of my fitting room. The next second they were wrenched aside and a nervous-looking woman in a print dress and carpet slippers, and with a row of pins sticking out of the corner of her mouth, burst into the room. Heaps of white organdy billowed over her right arm. A fat red pin cushion with more pins in it was strapped to her left wrist.

"Is it this child?" she bawled over her left shoulder into the corridor. She was very careful to keep the corner of her mouth with the pins in it closely

 66

pressed together. No one answered. She turned to me looking slightly desperate.

"Are you the child? What are you supposed to be anyway?"

I supposed she meant in the bridal show. "A graduated flower girl, number four," I said, proud of remembering Monique's last-minute information given to me in the car.

"A or B?" the pin-lady wanted to know.

"A or B?"

"Yes. Very important. I have to know. Are you going to be on the left side of the procession or the right side? The sleeve ruching and the draped swathes have to go either to the left or the right, so that they're on the outside as you pass down the aisle."

"Oh," I said, "like mirror images."

"Yeah. Sort of."

"Well, I don't know. Nobody told me."

The pin-lady groaned. "Don't anybody do *nothing* right around here? How'm I supposed to know? All right. Look, meanwhile try this on. Come on. Take your clothes off."

I was hoping she'd go while I undressed. But she didn't. She stood there, repeatedly shaking the mass of white organdy in front of her, like a bullfighter trying to attract the attention of a bull, while I wriggled out of my shirt and dungarees.

A moment later, like Angelica in the next dressing room (which had gone dead quiet, by the way) my head was muffled in yards of material. It finally got past my nose and mouth. The pin-lady was down on her knees pulling and tugging. "Oh, my God," she groaned. "Never."

She got up, pulled aside the curtain, and bawled out into the corridor again. "Miss Hawkins!" Someone must have appeared at the end of the corridor. "Tell Miss Hawkins, *right now,* please. I haven't got all night. In three minutes I'm going on relief, overtime pay or not. What a day!"

The pin-lady must have been more important than she looked because Cheryl Hawkins appeared in about five seconds. Monique's mother's friend, the Blair & Harper fashion consultant, was pretty scary, with black-eye make-up in panda-like rings around her eyes and dark-red hair done up in stiff corkscrews all over her head like an angry Greek goddess. An extremely long fingernail held the curtain to one side as she stood in the entry of the dressing room.

"Miss Hawkins," the pin-lady said exasperatedly. "I can't make this fit. This is a four A or four B flower girl, and she's all belly fat. Do you or don't you want me to custom a dress for her? I've got to know right now."

"Turn around slowly, dear," Cheryl Hawkins said,

 68

flashing a fingernail in my direction.

I did.

"Goblin-shaped," Miss Hawkins muttered while my back was turned. "How old are you, dear?" she asked in a brightly unnatural voice when I'd completed the turn and stood facing her.

"Eleven and a half. I'll be twelve in November."

The pin-lady prodded me with a fist. "Baby fat," she said, "all baby fat around the middle. No waist at all."

"Immature figure," Miss Hawkins mumbled, as if to herself. She turned to the pin-lady. "Don't do anything yet. We're still waiting for the other number four girl. She was supposed to have been here tonight but she hasn't shown up." She glanced at her watch.

The pin-lady drew herself to her full height and wrenched the pins out of the corner of her mouth. "Well, that tears it. I'm going on relief." She whipped the billows of organdy off my head in one grand swoop and stalked past Miss Hawkins and down the corridor.

I stood there in my underwear. "What should I do?"

"Get dressed," Miss Hawkins snapped. I couldn't tell if she was angry at me or at the pin-lady or at the other number four flower girl who hadn't shown up.

69

"And what then?"

"Wait here. If the other girl shows I'll let you know. I can't even run a rehearsal tonight. Nobody's *here!*" The fingernail withdrew, the curtain dropped, and Miss Hawkins vanished.

I finished dressing and sat down on the pink plastic stool again. 'Belly fat!' 'Goblin-shaped!' 'Immature figure!' Really! What was I anyway? A prize piglet at the county fair? This was impossible. I got up and left the fitting room to try to find Monique. If the other number four girl arrived and they wanted me, they could just yell.

I found Monique at last in a giant sewing room with six or seven sewing machines, ironing boards, tall racks for hanging clothes, and lots of wooden and plastic manikins. She was standing near a sewing table in a floating white dress while a dark-skinned young woman with lustrous black hair knelt at her feet sewing tiny appliques of pale shell-pink rosebuds to the hem.

"Oh, there you are," I said with relief to the back of Monique's head. Monique didn't turn around.

"All set?" she said, sounding as though she was barely moving her lips.

"No," I said disgustedly, sitting down on a wooden bench full of straight pins. "The dress doesn't fit me, the other number four flower girl isn't here, and there isn't going to be any rehearsal tonight because

 70

not enough people showed up."

"Never mind," Monique said, in the same tight-lipped voice. "You'll get paid anyway."

I nodded. But it all seemed pretty silly, the way Blair & Harper wasted their money. I sat there watching the rosebud operation until it was finished. Then Monique went to get dressed and phone Geraldine to come and get us, and to check with Cheryl Hawkins about her final fitting and her rehearsal schedule.

Miss Hawkins was off somewhere in one of the fitting rooms. (Maybe she'd been called in to settle the cream-versus-eggshell argument.)

When Monique came back, she and I just sat there among the tailor's dummies and didn't say much, although Monique's lips were moving slightly. She was silently mouthing the 'firecracker' cheer and making sharp little jerks and thrusts and half-jabs with her head, arms, knees, and feet.

All of a sudden Cheryl Hawkins clattered into the sewing room. It had no carpet and her heels made a terrific staccato racket on the wooden floor.

"So?" she said, black panda eyes darting from us to the dummies and back again.

"So my dress is just about finished," Monique said, examining one of her fingernails. "When's the first rehearsal?"

Miss Hawkins looked at her watch. It was enor-

71

mous with a wide, shiny, green plastic band. I guess it was a calendar watch because her head shot up immediately. "Next Thursday at six P.M. For a final fitting and a complete rehearsal."

"And what about her?" Monique asked, poking an elbow in my direction because she was still fiddling with the fingernail.

Miss Hawkins opened her eyes a little wider as though she was slightly exasperated at having just been asked a stupid question. "Both of you."

But I just *had* to be sure. "Both?" I swallowed.

"Both," she said, losing interest and rushing over to one of the manikins to rearrange a flounce on a satin skirt.

I looked at Monique and breathed a sigh of relief. I guess I was still in the bridal show, belly fat and all.

It was only about seven o'clock when I walked in the house.

"That you, Cress?" It was my mother's voice. The next moment she was at the top of the entry stairs with some clothes thrown over her right arm, almost but not quite like the Blair & Harper pin-lady.

"Well, where've you been gallivanting?"

"Didn't Dad tell you?"

"Yes, in fact he did."

"So?" I headed toward my room going past Dad's

 72

study and noticing that the door was closed which meant he was working.

"What's wrong, Cress? You seem upset."

Mom followed me to my room. I plunked down on the edge of the bed. "What are the clothes for?"

Mom laughed and threw them over the back of a chair. "Oh just some things I've been getting ready to pack. I've got to leave in the morning. It came up very suddenly. One of the conference delegates was stricken with appendicitis this afternoon. I've got to go in her place."

"Where to?"

"Minneapolis. It's an important regional meeting, with two Eastern delegates pledged to attend, so I'll have to be one of them."

I leaned back on my elbows. "Monique's mother left for Palm Beach this morning. She's organizing a big fashion show down there for charity."

My mother smiled. "I think I'd rather help put new thoughts into women's minds than new clothes on their backs. So tell me, what happened at Blair & Harper?"

"Oh nothing much. I've got a fitting and a rehearsal next Thursday at six P.M."

Mom laughed.

"What's funny?"

"Nothing really. It just sounds peculiar, Cressie, hearing words like that from you. Did you enjoy it?"

73

"Well not much happened tonight, so I can't say yet."

Mom leaned over and patted my arm as though she was forgiving me for some silly thing I'd done. "Okay, you try it and let me know. I'm afraid you'll find it's pretty dull and pointless work."

"They're paying me," I said defensively.

"Money isn't the measure of things," Mom said. The words came out of her almost automatically.

I didn't say anything.

"What's wrong, Cress? You seem unhappy about something. Look, I'll be gone for four or five days. You better tell me what's the matter."

"Well. . . ." It was hard to begin. "I've got homework," I said, making a quick lunge toward the school books on my desk.

"Not just now. Sit down. Come on, I want to hear all about it."

"Well," I began again, "it's your not liking or approving of anything I do. Or liking my friends or . . . or, people I like."

Mom leaned forward. "Could you make that a little clearer, Cress?"

I picked at a thumb nail and didn't look up.

"Okay. Let's start with this fashion-modeling thing. You know why I disapprove of it. I don't think women should be slaves to fashion. Fashions are only passing fads to make money for business

 74

interests. When a woman or girl concentrates too much on clothing and appearance, she doesn't usually take much notice of really important issues. But don't get me wrong. It's perfectly okay for you to do this bridal show, Cress. I think you'll learn something from it. Come on, what else is there?"

There were so many things. There were the new names on the mailbox yesterday afternoon which she had talked me into believing was a great idea and which had nearly gotten me into an all-out battle with Davey. There was her not wanting me to "wait" on Davey or bake cookies for him which I really loved to do. There was the way she had treated Xandra which I was so upset over I couldn't even talk about it. And now there was the fact that she was going to be away over the weekend and leave Dad and me alone again.

"Well," I blurted at last, "you embarrass me in front of my friends."

"How?"

"In front of Davey Link. Just yesterday. You know those new names you put on the letterbox? He actually thought they were an April Fools' joke. If you must know, Davey thought it meant that you and Dad had gotten divorced!"

Mom closed her eyes and laughed. "But you knew about that, Cress. We discussed it beforehand and you said yourself you thought it made perfect sense."

"Well, it didn't make any kind of sense when I tried explaining it to Davey."

"Think of it this way," Mom said, with that unchanging smile on her face. "When a woman puts aside her name to take the name of the man she marries, it seems to say she was not really very important or worthwhile unmarried. She had no guaranteed permanent identity as a 'single' person. But men keep the names they were born with all their lives. They'd be horrified to have them changed by marriage. Haven't you ever heard the jokes they make about men who are married to very famous women? Let's say a famous movie actress. It's considered the worst kind of insult when her husband is referred to as *Mr.* Gloria Glamorpuss, or whatever. But a woman who's called Mrs. Philip Richardson isn't supposed to mind a bit. Well, I do. I love your father, but I do. One thing hasn't anything to do with the other."

Mom's arguments were so logical, she got me annoyed. "Well, speaking of names," I said sulkily, "why in the world did you ever give me a nothing name like Cress? People always want to know what it's short for. They don't even know what I'm supposed to be. And if I have to go on and on explaining your ideas to my friends, they're really going to think I'm peculiar."

Mom began to lift her clothes off the back of the

chair so she could take them back to her room to pack them.

"Cress is not a 'nothing' name," she said, very calmly. "It's an 'everything' name, which is exactly why I gave it to you. If you think about that for a while, I'm sure you'll know what I mean."

"Look," I shouted, a little astonished to find myself screaming but going on with it just the same, "I hate riddles and I hate the stupid names you keep thinking up. And I don't want to have to listen to any more of your ideas. They make me sick. I don't care about 'women's liberation' and all that . . . fluff! I just want to be left alone. I want to be . . . me!"

Mom tossed her things over her shoulder, got as far as the doorway, and turned and looked at me with a surprised smile on her face.

"Why, Cress, how did you guess? That's exactly who I want you to be." Then she went out and softly closed the door behind her.

I banged my fists on the mattress until the bed began to bounce. I was furious. You could simply never win an argument with my mother. Why, you couldn't even *have* an argument with my mother.

7

 Friday morning Mom left for Minneapolis, and Friday evening I baked cookies like mad. Three different kinds, all chocolate. Naturally, that was because chocolate was what Davey liked best.

Saturday was going to be a perfect day for the lake. It was a crazy April, all right, in more ways than one. The weather reporters on TV and radio kept saying how "unseasonably" warm it was for this early in spring. And one forecaster with a very long face, on the six o'clock news, had actually called it a "false spring." But I wasn't letting him dampen my enthusiasm.

The way Davey and I had arranged it, we were going to meet at the supermarket very early on Saturday morning, pick up all the sandwich fixings, and then bicycle directly to the lake where we'd meet all the others.

Davey was already waiting in front of the Giant Superfood store in the shopping center when I got there.

78

"Here's the list," he said, thrusting a piece of ruled looseleaf paper at me the minute I got close enough.

I got off my bike and started to read it. Sure enough, he wanted corned beef (very lean), rye bread (without caraway seeds), mustard (mild yellow), potato salad (with lots of mayonnaise), potato chips (the crinkly kind), and for pickles he wanted 'kosher dill gherkins.'

"I never heard of those," I said, pointing to the last item on the list.

"That's the only kind I like with corned beef. Oh . . . and here." Davey shot a five-dollar bill into my hand. "I'll stay out here and mind the bikes and the fishing gear. And don't dawdle, Cress."

"What's that supposed to mean?"

"Oh, you know the way women waste time in supermarkets, squeezing the bread, sniffing into the jars of salad dressing."

I snorted. "About this list," I said, waving the page at Davey, "you never said how *much* I should get."

"Oh," Davey responded absently, peering into the basket fastened to the front of my bike and beginning to poke around, for the cookies no doubt, "get enough."

"How much is enough? How many are going to be there?"

79

"Besides us? Oh . . . about three. Two or three."

I glanced at the five-dollar bill doubtfully. "Delicatessen corned beef is pretty expensive, Davey. Of course, I do have a little money with me. . . ."

Davey triumphantly pulled a chocolate drop-cookie out of one of the boxes wrapped in the plastic bag that was sitting in my basket. "Oh, no," he chomped with his mouth full, "I couldn't ask you to do that, Cress. Not after you baked all these terrific cookies. Anyhow, you don't really need to worry about the other guys."

"You mean they're bringing their own?"

"Yeah. Sort of."

I shrugged and marched into Superfood. It really was a giant store. The aisles were so long that when you looked down them they narrowed at the far end, like tunnels. But it was already pretty crowded. I guess the warm weather had started everybody thinking about picnics and cookouts. Even pool parties.

Everything took a little longer than it usually did. While I was standing on line at the delicatessen counter with a ticket marked number 96 (and the clerks were only up to number 82), Davey came waddling impatiently into the store. He'd met a boy he knew outside and had asked him to watch the bikes for a minute or two. Sure enough Davey was chewing on a Toll House cookie this time.

"Gee you're taking an awfully long time, Cress."

"I can't help it," I hissed, holding up my number ticket. "All these people got here before me while you were keeping me out on the sidewalk telling me not to dawdle and *not* telling me how much corned beef I should get. And I *still* don't know how much I should get."

Davey simply popped the rest of the cookie into his mouth and disappeared, warning me to be sure to get the right kind of pickles.

At last I finished the shopping. We piled the stuff into my basket and some into Davey's saddlebags, and set off for Grover's Lake. I had spent two and a half dollars of my own money, but I didn't say anything just then. I figured we could straighten out all the expenses when we got to the lake.

It was about a six-mile ride, not very uphill, but my bike was loaded with groceries. (I had the corned beef, the bread, the potato salad, the kosher dill gherkins, *and* the cookies, while Davey had the mustard, the potato chips, and the fishing rods.) Thank goodness, Davey had told Rodge and the others to bring the Cokes.

I was beet-faced and sweating, and Davey was getting a pretty good lead on me. Every now and then he'd stop and wait for me to nearly catch up. Then he'd call out over his shoulder without turning around, "Come on, Cress. Put a little more muscle into it." Then he'd speed ahead again, leaving

81

me behind. I was too winded to answer him but I kept thinking of the words in that cheer Monique was always practicing lately:

"The boys have the muscles,
The coach has the brains,
The girls have the sexy legs
To win all the games!"

I didn't have sexy legs, but I didn't have the muscles either. I figured I wasn't doing badly, though. The reason Davey and the boys had asked me to their secret hideout at Grover's Lake was because they liked *me* as a person. And that was a really nice compliment. I felt proud. I think it was on the strength of that that I finally got my second wind and managed to arrive neck in neck with Davey at the turnoff to the lake.

We had to get off our bikes and walk them through the underbrush for about 150 yards, and just before we came out into the clearing around the lake we heard voices.

It wasn't a very big lake. Actually it was more of a pond. And the voices we'd heard were coming from out in the middle of it where three boys, Roger Hollister and two others, sat in a funny, old, flat-bottomed rowboat. They all had fishing rods, the lines dangling into the quiet sun-dappled water.

"Hey, guys!" Davey yelled.

Roger stood up in the boat and began waving his arms, not in greeting, but to tell Davey to pipe down, probably because he was scaring the fish.

But Davey paid no attention. "Come on over here and get me," he shouted. He turned to me. "That's the only boat we've got. We patched it up real good last fall and kept it hidden in the woods all winter wrapped in a tarpaulin."

"How many can it hold?" I asked. "Safely, that is."

" 'Bout three or four," Davey answered, squinting as he watched Rodge start paddling toward us with what looked like a very short oar. In fact, it probably was a canoe paddle.

"So how can five of us get in?" I wanted to know.

Davey scratched his head. "I didn't think Brad and Chet would *both* show up, to tell you the truth. Uh, maybe we'll take turns, Cress. First one group'll go out fishing, say for about three-quarters of an hour, and then another group'll go. Why don't I go this first time, Cress? Just to try it. Make sure the boat's not leaking and all that."

I nodded. Davey's suggestion seemed to make sense. The only thing I didn't like about it was having to stay behind on shore with Roger, who hadn't been acting any too friendly the last couple of times I'd seen him, or with Brad or Chet whom I

83

didn't know. What would I find to talk to them about?

Davey began unfastening his fishing gear from his bike, while Roger paddled the boat closer and closer.

"Look around for worms, Cress. See any worms?"

"Oh, for God's sake, Davey," I said. "You expect them to be just lying around here and waiting? Didn't you bring any bait?"

"Not really," he muttered. "Rodge probably has some."

Roger was paddling faster now, almost furiously, his head bent very low. The moment he got into shallow enough water he jumped out of the boat, barefoot, and pulled it up onto the mud to beach it. Then he straightened up, looked at me with no smile of any kind, and murmured "Hi," as he quickly stepped past me to Davey who was now setting up his fishing rod.

"You're late, you know, fella. Think it's fun having to row that old tub back here without even an oar?"

Davey looked up at Roger with a grin. "Are they biting?"

"How should I know? We only just got there and got our lines in the water when you came along and started screaming 'Come and get me'." Roger mimicked Davey's voice which was very high-pitched

 84

compared to Roger's extra-deep one. Then Roger's voice dropped to a thick whisper. "What's *she* doing here?"

I could see Davey's cheek flush. "I told you," he said very softly. "Said I might bring somebody along."

Roger bent lower over Davey. "You never said *who*. I figured it would be a guy."

I went away and sat down in a spot a little farther up the bank where it was grassy instead of muddy. The two boys in the beached boat just stared across at me and I stared back. They seemed younger than Roger, closer to Davey's age. They both had wavy brown hair and smooth 'pretty' faces with pink cheeks. The only difference between them seemed to be that one wore thick-looking glasses. I couldn't tell if they were brothers or not.

As I sat there thinking about what I'd just over-heard, and digesting the fact that Davey had never even told Roger and the others that he was bringing me along, Davey marched into the boat, just like some admiral going aboard a battleship, and settled himself in the bow. "Ahoy there, Cress," he shouted, as if he were already halfway out to sea. "In a little while you can start making up the sandwiches, get all the food ready. You know, for when we get back."

"Yeah," Roger added, grinning as he headed toward the rowboat. "And watch out for bears behind you. The woods are full of 'em!''

I scrambled to my feet, scowling furiously, and started down the grassy slope toward the shore. Roger turned and held up one hand like a traffic cop. "Don't bother yourself there, ma'am. Don't need any lady welders for this job. I can push her off all right." He took a running start, shoved the boat off the mud into the water, and leaped aboard.

My mouth must have been wide open. Lady welders! Of course Roger had overheard my conversation with Mr. Grinnell about getting into the metal-sculpture club. But what ever made him think I wanted to help *him* with anything?

I wanted to shout back all sorts of things at Roger, at Davey, and at those two wordless creatures, Brad and Chet, who had now broken out into sly grins. Like Davey, they seemed to think everything Roger said and did was great. Why didn't Roger find some friends his own age instead of putting on his big brother act with younger kids?

With everything hitting me at once, I couldn't think of one single thing to say. All I knew was the four boys were now going off fishing together, leaving me behind to play 'mother.'

Well, did I or didn't I want the part? Sure, I didn't mind baking cookies and making sandwiches and all that. In fact, I liked it. But it wasn't going to take me that long to set out the lunch. Why

 86

couldn't Brad or Chet, or Roger himself, have stayed behind this time and let me go out fishing with Davey? After all, I was Davey's guest.

I was feeling hurt and grumpy but somehow the next hour went by faster than I thought it would. I found the Cokes Roger and the others had brought and put the bottles into the water near the edge of the pond, under a flat rock in a patch of shade, so they'd be icy cold by lunchtime. Then I began to set out a really nice picnic on the grass, using the plastic tablecloth and the fancy paper plates and cups and napkins that I'd brought along.

While hunting for the Cokes, I noticed that Roger and the others had also brought along a couple of packages of frankfurters and some boxes of marshmallows. So I started searching around for green sticks on which we could grill the hot dogs and toast the marshmallows.

I had just finished gathering a pile of dry twigs and branches for starting the cooking fire when I noticed that the rowboat had begun heading in toward shore. I really hated the idea of sitting around at a picnic with Roger Hollister. But maybe he'd begin acting a little nicer toward me when he saw the food laid out and saw how I'd chilled the Cokes and arranged the wood for the fire.

The moment Davey got ashore he handed me a tiny fish, about the size of a canned sardine, and made a beeline for the picnic food.

"Is this bait or what?" I called out after him. The poor little thing looked like it had been dead for days.

"No, it's not bait," Davey answered indignantly. "That's what I caught. That's *all* I caught. Roger got one a little bigger and Brad got one about the same size as mine. But they both threw them back. I only brought this so I could show you how they're just not biting today. Rodge says it's too early in the season."

"Never mind," I said consolingly, as I walked over to Davey. "When you and I go out after lunch we'll have better luck."

Brad and Chet had come over to look at the picnic food and were milling around and glancing down at it appreciatively. They both said "hi" to me, and Davey told me which was Brad and which was Chet. Chet was the one with the glasses. Neither one had much else to say, but I decided they were probably okay. Just shy.

Roger took a long time with the boat and when he had pulled it far up on the beach he sat down on the edge of it and put on his sneakers. When he finally joined the rest of us he was shaking his head. "She sure is taking water," he said with a very serious air.

I looked toward Davey. "The boat's leaking?"

 88

Davey looked over at Roger and Roger nodded back to Davey. "Sure is," Roger said. "She's finished for today. Got to do a whole lot of patching next time we come out here."

I ignored Roger. He didn't seem to be talking to me, so I kept on talking to Davey. "How much water?"

Davey cleared his throat, still looking over at Roger. "Oh, a lot. We had to bail."

"That's funny," I remarked. "I didn't see anybody bailing out there. And you stayed out so long. Over an hour."

"You could never see us bailing from here," Roger challenged. "What are you doing? Calling us liars? Why don't you go take a look for yourself?"

I walked down to the boat and peered in. There was only a tiny bit of water in the bottom, in one small place. The rest of the inside of the boat didn't even look wet. What was Roger talking about?

I marched back confidently. "It'll be okay. Anyhow, I can swim real well. And if you're really worried, Davey, we'll stay close to shore."

Davey shook his head. "I don't know, Cress. It might be risky. And anyhow, I told you, the fish just aren't biting today. There's nothing to catch."

"Okay then," I said. "I'll go out myself. You invited me here to go fishing and that's what I'll do. Right after lunch."

89

Roger stood there, arms folded across his chest. His eyes were fixed on the ground. "Not in our boat, you won't, girlie."

"Girlie!"

The corners of Roger's mouth curled into a sinister smile. "Something wrong?"

Before I could even answer him he strolled away, stopping short in front of the mound of twigs I'd arranged for the fire. "What's this?" he asked, over his shoulder.

"What does it look like?" I shot back.

"Doesn't look like anything to me," he said. And with one kick of his foot he sent the carefully arranged twigs and branches flying.

Glowering, my fists clenched at my sides, I took a few steps toward Roger. "Why did you do that?" I demanded in a tight voice.

Roger answered by ignoring me completely and talking above my head to the three boys. "Thinks she knows how to build a fire," he snickered. "Thinks she can handle a boat all by herself. Some dame. Now *she's* what you call a real know-it-all."

Furious, I whirled around, facing Davey and the others, my back to Roger. "I might not know *everything*," I said, mocking Roger bitterly, "but there's one thing I do know. I'm not sticking around here another second!" And, blazing with anger, I made for the fringe of trees where I'd left my bike.

 90

I could hear Davey following behind me, muttering something like, "Calm down, Cress. What are you getting so excited about?" And I could hear suppressed giggles from Brad and Chet. I was glad I couldn't see the ugly triumphant grin that must have been spreading all over Roger's face.

In an instant I was on my bike. But Davey rushed over and grabbed the handlebars. "Aw, come on, Cress. Quit it."

"Listen, Davey," I said, staring him straight in the eyes, "I understand now exactly why you invited me here today." I pointed to the picnic, all beautifully laid out on the grass—corned beef sandwiches, pickles, potato salad, home-baked chocolate cookies (three kinds), the works. "And there it is. So eat it!"

And, sweeping Davey's hands off the handlebars, I crashed off into the underbrush, vines and branches snapping in my face.

But Davey was huffing and puffing behind me on foot. My bike hit a sharp rock and swerved, and I had to stop a moment to right myself. Davey caught up.

"Look, Cress," he gasped, red-faced, "I know Roger didn't act exactly . . . nice to you . . . just now. But what are you so mad at *me* for?"

"What am I mad at *you* for! You don't know, huh? You really don't know? Well, all right. Since you're so dumb and innocent, I'll tell you. I'm mad at you for lying to me in the first place, for breaking your promise to me in the second place, and for treating me like I'm some kind of a . . . a slave!"

"But, Cress, I didn't. . . ."

"Oh, no? I'll tell you what you *didn't* do. You didn't tell Roger and those other two that you were bringing me along. You kind of 'sneaked' me in, figuring it would be all right and they'd let me stay because of the nice lunch I'd fix. Then you arranged with Roger to say the boat was leaking. I was good enough to fix lunch but not good enough to go fishing or even row around the lake in your stupid old boat. Or even to build a fire for Roger's precious hot dogs. . . ."

Davey began to back away. "Listen here, Cress," he said, partly as if he was frightened and partly as though he was warning me, "I think you're acting kind of crazy. If you must know, I've been thinking it ever since April Fools' Day. It's that family of yours. It's got something to do with your mother. You better watch out. I'm not kidding."

"You leave my mother out of it!" I snapped. I had gotten off my bike because I knew I'd have to walk it the rest of the way out of the woods. "Just go eat your lunch, Davey."

Davey looked bewildered for a moment. "But aren't you going to have any? I mean, look at all

 92

those sandwiches you made. And the cookies. . . ."

"*You* eat the cookies, Davey. You and Roger, and
. . . and Chad and Bret . . . or whatever those
two kids' names are. You eat them, all of you. And
I hope you all . . . *choke!*"

I was nearly halfway home, peddling madly along
the road we'd come on, when I remembered about
the Cokes, submerged under the big flat stone in
the shallows of the pond. Roger and Davey and the
two dimwits would never find them in a million
years. The wettest thing they'd have for lunch would
be pickle juice. And as for their choking—which
would have been a very big satisfaction to me at the
time—well, there was a very good chance that they
would!

8

I decided I wasn't on speaking terms anymore with Davey Link. Altogether it was a terrible
weekend, with Mom away and Dad trying to act
cheery and find things for us to do together when
he wasn't catching up on paperwork in his study.

Of course, Mom's being off in Minneapolis that
Saturday afternoon was the best thing that could
have happened. If she'd been home, she would have
found out in no time at all about my big blow-up
with Davey. And she would have said 'I told you
so.' Oh, not in so many words, of course. But smil-
ingly and tactfully, and very pointedly, she would
have shown me how Davey had been "using" me because he was a glutton and because he was looking
for a "little mother" to fuss over him, not for a
friend and a companion.

Dad, on the other hand, didn't seem to notice my
moping much. I guess he thought I was acting that
way because Mom was away over a weekend. Anyhow, Dad's mind must have been on business about

 94

ninety-six per cent of the time.

When I got on the school bus on Monday morning, I just turned and faced front quickly and dropped into the first empty seat. I never knew if Davey was on the bus or not, but there was a good chance he was. Probably even Roger, too. I did the same thing on Tuesday and Wednesday.

On Wednesday afternoon, just after I got home from school, a package arrived by parcel post. I gasped because the return address was Davey's, and I tore it open a lot more eagerly than I should have, considering how cold I felt toward him. At last I got the heavy brown paper off and saw what was inside.

It was just like Davey to pack up the plastic tablecloth and the leftover paper plates and napkins from the picnic and mail them back to me. I guess he figured the cups were too bulky to wrap because he left them out. Or maybe he and Roger and the others had found the Cokes after all and used up all the cups. Also, I noticed Davey didn't send me back any of the cookies (which he definitely must have eaten, guilty conscience or not) or the two and a half dollars that he didn't even know he owed me.

There was also a note in the package. It gave me a sick feeling when I saw it flutter out and fall to the floor with Davey's squiggly, wavering handwriting all over it. Here's what the note said:

95

Well, Cress, it's too bad about what happened between us. I thought your mother might need the tablecloth so I am packing it up with the other things and mailing it to you. Even if our friendship is busted up, it was a very good lunch. And especially the chocolate cookies.

I guess you'll keep on not talking to me. But anyhow I want to wish you luck in the fashion show and hope you are a very big success. As you probably know, I'll be leaving for naval academy prep school in September.

Very truly yours,
David James Peter Link III

P.S. Roger thinks somebody stole the Cokes when he and the fellows stopped at a gas station on their way to the lake to get air in Chet's bicycle tire. Anyhow, we didn't have anything to drink at the picnic.

I didn't know whether to laugh or cry. If only Davey wasn't friends with Roger Hollister, I think I would have gone to the phone and called him up right then and there. It was nice of him to wish me luck in the fashion show. On the other hand, I couldn't forget how he had tricked me about going to the lake. And he hadn't even apologized for that! It was just something I was supposed to accept.

I got so restless and irritable thinking about the mess with Davey that I decided I'd phone Xandra up at school. It was a week since her visit. I suppose I just wanted to talk to somebody warm and sym-

 96

pathetic, even if I didn't exactly talk to her about Davey.

I was lucky. Xandra was in her dorm room and she picked up the phone right away.

"Cress!" she said, sounding pleased. "How've you been?"

"Well, okay. A lot's been happening around here. I was wondering how you . . . and Bill . . . were. Mom's away. She left last Friday and she's coming back tonight. Some conference in Minneapolis."

"Oh, oh," Xandra laughed. "That's how come you're calling. Cat's away."

"What?"

"Nothing. I'm sorry. So what are all these things that are happening?"

I told her about my being in the Blair & Harper bridal show and she fairly screeched with delight.

"Oh, Cressie, I'd love to be able to see you in that."

"Well, you can. It's going to be at the end of the month. Promise you'll come."

"I'd like to, Cress. Really I would. But you see there are exams and there's so much to do, what with the wedding plans. . . ."

"Oh, the wedding! What about the wedding, Xandra?"

"Ours? Oh, it's going to be a modest affair. Nothing like the kind of thing Blair & Harper puts on.

Not a single flower girl even. If there were one, it would definitely be you."

"Maybe I could come anyway. As a guest. Or a . . . a witness? Where's it going to be and when?"

"Back home. In Arizona. The second week in June."

My voice dropped. "School won't even be finished by then. How could I?"

"Well, look, don't fret. You'll see us before we leave for Ireland. Somehow."

"How about Easter?" I asked brightly. "That's only a week away."

"Uh-uh. Bill and I are driving out to Wisconsin so his parents can meet me. I'm pretty nervous."

"Oh don't be, Xandra. They'll love you just like I do. Especially when they think of all you're doing for Bill. . . ." I paused, imagining Mom's reaction to that idea. "But if you can't come for Easter, I really hope you can come to the fashion show so you can see me dressed as a flower girl. It's such a dreamy outfit."

"Cress honey, I'm sure it is. But I just can't promise. In fact, I'm going to have to say goodbye right now. So listen, you be a happy bunny. And if I don't make it to the bridal show, I wish you loads of luck and I hope you're a very big success in it!"

"A very big success." Funny. That was exactly what Davey had said in his note.

When Mom got home from Minneapolis later that evening (looking tired and straggly even though she said she was happy and excited), I didn't say anything to her about my phone call to Xandra. I just knew Xandra wouldn't be coming to the bridal show and I couldn't help feeling that if Mom hadn't been so sour to her about dropping out of school to get married, I would be seeing a lot more of her before she went away for good.

The very next day was Thursday and I was due at Blair & Harper that evening. "Six P.M. for a final fitting and a complete rehearsal," Cheryl Hawkins had said.

Of course, I hadn't even had my *first* fitting yet. But hopefully the other number four flower girl would be there this time, and the pin-lady would be able to get our white organdy dresses with the sleeve ruching and the draped swathes under way. I wondered if I would be a four A or a four B flower girl, and I studied my profile in the three-way medicine-cabinet mirror a few times trying to decide which side was better. Just in case I had a choice.

Geraldine, grumbling as usual about the chauffeuring, drove Monique and me to the Blair & Harper store. When we got there, we were surprised to find out that we were late. The rehearsal time had been changed to 5:30 but somehow the message had never been received at Monique's house. Anyhow, this time everyone was gathered in the Blair & Harper third-floor restaurant which was called 'The Pecan Tree.'

There wasn't a pecan tree in sight, just a lot of small white tables with small white wicker chairs stacked on top of them. There were murals painted on the walls of the restaurant, though, showing southern gardens with vine-covered arbors, river scenes with paddle steamers, and old southern mansions, not too different from Monique's. I suppose it was a nice gentle setting for Blair & Harper's lady shoppers to have lunch or afternoon tea in.

But now the tables had been pushed toward the sides of the room, leaving a broad open space that slanted diagonally from the cashier's desk at the customer's entrance all the way to the kitchen entrance. This was going to be the display aisle for the bridal procession, both in rehearsal and at the regular showings. "Except, of course, for the showings we'll be up higher," Monique whispered, "on a platform with ramps off to the sides so some of the models can walk out into the audience." The whole idea made my stomach do a flip-flop.

Cheryl Hawkins really meant what she said about having a "complete" rehearsal this time, because there were an awful lot of people around. Miss Hawkins looked even more fierce than the last time.

 100

She clapped her hands and the noise sounded like a shot. She was standing up on a makeshift board platform, about three steps high, and I couldn't help noticing that this time she had on green nail polish and a wide, shiny, *orange* plastic watchband.

"Some of you are late!" she said, panda eyes flashing. "I want you to take your places in the bridal procession now. Miss Carbone will call out your designations. We'll begin with the bridesmaids. No talking, please."

If I closed my eyes, Miss Hawkins reminded me exactly of one of those very strict, old-fashioned schoolteachers that you read about in books or see sometimes in movies or on TV.

Miss Carbone was quite different from Miss Hawkins. She was a small, dark-haired woman with a soft voice and an earnest expression. Monique said she was head of costuming and Miss Hawkins' assistant. Some of the models were wearing bits and pieces of their bridal costumes, so it was easy to tell who they were. The eight bridesmaids all had on floppy ruffled organza hats, the color of pale orange sherbet. Otherwise they were dressed in pants outfits, or short skirts with high plastic boots, or whatever they happened to be wearing that day. Monique said they had all been sent from a model agency in New York City, and it was easy to imagine any one of them stepping quite naturally into the satiny

101

pages of *Chic* and remaining there forever in a pose of frozen glamor.

Standing off to one side was the bride, a honey blonde, even more gorgeous than the eight brides-maid models, and nearly as tall as Monique's mother. You could tell she was the bride, because she was wearing a great gauzy veil that billowed and wafted like pure white smoke for yards and yards behind her. Beneath this enormous white cloud she was dressed in a skin-hugging jersey top, blue jeans, and dirty sneakers.

Miss Carbone called up all the bridesmaids, the maid of honor, and the lead flower girl who was Monique, of course. Monique took her place in the procession, and then Miss Carbone began calling the pairs of flower girls.

First came the number ones, both streaky blondes, perfectly matched in height and just a notch or two shorter than Monique. I had a hunch they came from the model agency, too. The number two pair of flower girls had softly shining long brown hair that reminded me of Xandra's. My heart was pound-ing and I could feel my palms growing sweaty. Miss Carbone was getting awfully close to number four.

The number three girls turned out to be twins, with thick, curly, carroty red hair and ruddy freckled cheeks and noses. They were medium-short and just a little bit plump and babyish. Everyone smiled or

 102

nodded appreciatively as they took their places.

All the pairs of flower girls were so perfectly matched that I had begun to look around a little desperately for somebody who resembled me in size, shape, and coloring. I was still wondering who my partner might be when Miss Carbone, holding up her right hand and glancing toward the empty places behind the number threes said, in a voice that was much livelier and louder than before, "And now, last but not least . . . our number *four* flower girls!"

Just at that moment a large stout woman in a blue smock planted herself directly in front of me, blocking my path to the procession aisle. I stepped around her as quickly as I could, rushed toward the aisle, and nearly collided there with a short, dark-haired girl, almost exactly my height. The only difference was that she was terribly thin and pale, with great dark eyes and straight, gleaming hair that fitted her head like a cap of neat feathers, some short and some long.

"Oh, 'scuse me," I panted, catching my breath.

The girl didn't say anything, just stepped back as though to let me pass across the aisle to the other side.

But of course I didn't.

"I guess you're one of the number four flower girls," I said.

103

The girl looked at me wide-eyed. "That's right," she said in an emotionless voice.

"Well, I'm the other one. My name is Cress. Cress Richardson." The girl just continued to stare. "I'm the other number four flower girl," I repeated, wondering if she was stupid or something.

"You can't be," she said, not blinking and still with no expression in her voice or on her face.

"Why not? Why can't I be?"

"You can't be. Because *she* is." The girl pointed, without taking her eyes off me, to another girl who, I was pretty sure, had just at that moment appeared at her side. The second girl looked so exactly like the first girl that I couldn't help wondering if I'd suddenly developed double vision.

"But it's impossible," I said, completely baffled, to the second girl. "Who are you?"

The two girls answered in a single voice. "We're the Pellegrino sisters."

I wondered if they were a circus act or something.

"I'm Annette," added the first girl, doing a vague curtsey. "And I'm Marie," said the second girl.

"You're twins?" I asked.

"No," said Annette. "I told you. Sisters."

"You sure look alike. How old are you?"

"I'm thirteen and a half and she's twelve and a half," Annette stated flatly.

"You're both pretty small for your age."

"We know," they chorused. "Everyone in our family's small."

"Well," I said, "there's some mistake. Only one of you can be a number four flower girl because I'm the other one."

Marie leaned forward. "No, you aren't."

"I certainly am," I insisted. "Miss Hawkins told me so herself."

Both girls just stood there shaking their heads from side to side and looking at me with large mournful eyes. Behind us there was a great deal of rustling. The bride had been called into place and Miss Carbone was adjusting her veil, while Miss Hawkins was giving the bride directions as to how many paces she was to walk behind the last of the flower girls.

"Here, you two," Miss Hawkins said, firmly gripping the shoulders of the two Pellegrinos and dragging them into place directly behind the red-haired number three girls, "stand absolutely still. Right in this spot." At the same time, I was shoved completely to one side, outside the line of procession.

"Miss Hawkins," I began, "just a minute. . . ." But she had already dashed off and no one was listening to me. Instead, Miss Carbone began to approach, beaming and with an almost embarrassed smile on her face.

"Well," she said, familiarly, going directly over

105

to the Pellegrino sisters. "How goes it?" They both looked up at her and nodded solemnly. She bent down and squeezed their shoulders. "Your costumes will be *gorgeous*. You'll see."

"But there's a terrible mistake here," I protested. "*I'm* a number four flower girl."

Miss Carbone looked at me absently. "No you aren't, dearie." She put her arms completely around the two tiny Pellegrinos. "These girls are. They're my nieces," she added proudly. "Lovely little girls. So clever, too."

"I don't care if they're atomic physicists," I said furiously. "You can't show favoritism like that. Wait till Miss Hawkins hears about this."

"Hears about what?" A green fingernail lay on my wrist. "I've been looking all over for you," she said impatiently. "Where've you been? Never mind. This is where you belong in the procession."

A warm happy flush came over me. This would teach the Pellegrinos and their loving aunt, Miss Carbone. I moved in closer to where the two sisters stood.

"Not *there,*" Miss Hawkins said in an agonized voice, grabbing me by the shoulder and pulling me back about two feet. Then she centered me directly behind the two Pellegrinos.

"But what am I?" I asked, looking up at her in

 106

bewilderment. "A number five flower girl?"

"Lord, no," she groaned. "We've got enough flower girls."

I looked around. Behind me stood the bride, smiling vacantly in her jeans, sneakers, and frothy white veil.

"You're the ring-bearer," Miss Hawkins said. "It's the first time we're having one, so you better not let us down," she warned.

"Oh, I won't," I promised, feeling pleased that, like Monique, I'd have a place to myself in the procession. "But you still didn't say what I'm supposed to do?"

Miss Hawkins drew her coral lips back from her teeth in what was almost a snarl. "Don't you know anything about weddings? You precede the bride down the aisle."

"Oh," I breathed, still not any too sure of my role.

"With the ring, the wedding ring, my dear, resting on a puffy little white satin cushion which you carry in your hands. You're a page, do you see?"

"Do you mean a boy page or a girl page?" I asked suspiciously.

"Pages," Miss Hawkins said coldly, "are usually boys. In real life, the ring-bearer might be the little brother or the nephew of the bride. And since you

107

have the rather 'cherubic' appearance of a plump, rosy-cheeked little boy, we think you'll do nicely for the part."

"I see," I said very slowly, beginning not to like the sound of this at all. "So if I'm definitely not going to be a flower girl, what kind of a costume will I wear?"

Miss Hawkins snapped her fingers for Miss Carbone who was now nearly halfway across the room but came running over at once. "Clara," Miss Hawkins said, "can you take this child away now for a costume fitting?"

Miss Carbone nodded eagerly. "Yes, I can. Oh . . . what did we decide on? Waistcoat or no waistcoat?"

"No waistcoat. Rose satin breeches. Tight. Ruffled white shirt. White stockings. Black patent shoes with large silver buckles. And remember," Miss Hawkins cautioned, patting first my too-protruding abdomen and then the back of me, "tight breeches. We want to make the most of that cherubic effect, don't you know."

For the first time I heard Miss Hawkins laugh. Actually it was more of a crackle, like the sound of dry leaves and twigs snapping under your feet. Or a thin sheet of peanut brittle being broken up into jagged, irregular pieces.

9

I stood miserably in dressing room number 37 in my underwear while Miss Carbone and two new pin-ladies fussed over me with tape measures and scissors, pieces of chalk and swatches of canvas cloth.

"Are you keeping your belly in on purpose?" one of the pin-ladies asked with narrowed eyes.

"No," I breathed.

She snapped the back of her hand smartly against my middle. "Well, let it out."

I suppose I was holding it in because when I looked down I saw it pop out another few notches.

"I wasn't doing it on purpose," I protested. "If I'm not fat enough for you, you could pad me with a pillow or something, you know."

"You're fat enough," the first pin-lady said drily. "And don't be a smarty."

"Better check all your measurements twice, Agnes," Miss Carbone cautioned. She was definitely trying to give the impression that I couldn't be trusted. The first pin-lady nodded and Miss Carbone left.

One of the pin-ladies had warts on her chin while the other one had three or four dark-colored moles on her cheek and jaw. I wondered if warts and moles were one of the hazards of their trade. Maybe if you stuck yourself with a pin enough times, a wart or a mole popped out.

After about half an hour of coming and goings, the two pin-ladies had me rigged out in a pair of rose satin knee breeches, held together at the seams with white basting thread.

"I'm having Carbone and Hawkins check on that," said the pin-lady called Agnes. "Not another stitch 'til they do." She beckoned to the second pin-lady. "Come along now, Madge."

"As for you," she said, giving me a threatening look, "stay right here until somebody comes. Don't budge."

"Don't worry," I promised. "I won't."

How could I? I was sewn into the breeches. They were skin-tight and they had no zipper or buttons yet to help me get out of them. In fact, I couldn't even sit down in them. All I could do was stand there and keep looking at my reflection in the mirror. It was horrid. From the waist up, I was dressed in my knitted white underwear top. From the waist down, I was all shiny and shimmering, all rose-colored bumps and bulges.

About five minutes passed and at last the dressing-room curtains parted. It was Monique. She was wearing her everyday clothes, meaning she had already had the final fitting of her flower-girl dress.

Monique stopped short in the entrance way, her hand flying to her mouth to try to stop a splutter of giggles.

"My God," she gulped. "I heard that you were going to be a page boy in the show. But what's *that?*"

"What's what?" I asked defiantly.

Monique came into the dressing room and began to walk around me slowly.

"Rose-colored tights, eh? What are they trying to do to you?"

"That's what I'd like to know," I said, accusingly. "You know, when you got me into this thing, you told me I was going to be a number four flower girl. And that's what I told everybody else I was going to be."

Monique took a deep breath. "Well, now don't blame me for that, sweetie. You know very well I'm not responsible. It's all up to Cheryl. At least I got you into the show, didn't I?"

"But just look at these awful pants," I shrilled.

111

"I thought I'd be dressed in some lovely long frilly dress, carrying a bouquet, looking really dreamy . . . and instead I get to impersonate some fat, dumb little boy carrying a pillow with a ring sitting on top of it. And these breeches. Miss Hawkins wants them so tight that I'm nearly bursting out of them."

Monique sat down on one of the little upholstered gilt chairs, crossed her legs, and put her chin in her hands. "Well, what do you want to do? Quit?"

"Just look at me. Don't you think I should?"

Monique shrugged. "And lose all the money you'd be getting? And after telling everyone you're in the show?"

"Well, I think it would be more embarrassing to stay in the show," I made a slow half-turn in front of the mirrors, "looking like this."

"Who's going to see you in the show? I mean who that you know? Probably the only person who'd come to it would be your mother."

"My mother! Are you kidding? My mother wouldn't be caught dead anywhere near a fashion show. She's all against that sort of thing."

"Well?" said Monique, "then what's to worry? You'd be a fool to back out of it now. All you have to do is just let everybody go on thinking you're what you said you were going to be in the first place —a flower girl. They won't ever need to know."

I stared at Monique. If I thought about that for a

 112

while, she was right. Davey, Xandra, my mother, even my father. None of them would ever need to know. I wouldn't be lying. I just wouldn't bother to tell them my part in the show had been changed. In the case of Davey, I remembered with a pang, it would be especially easy since I wasn't even talking to him anymore.

Monique got up from her chair and wagged a finger at me. "Because let me tell you something, Cress Richardson. If you do back out, don't ever expect me to do you any kind of a favor again. And it wouldn't help our friendship one little bit either. I made a lot of enemies among my other friends because of recommending you."

"Really?" I said, with an air of surprise. "I didn't know you had any other friends who were only four feet two."

Monique flashed a look at me and changed the subject. "What's taking so long anyway? I'd like to call Geraldine to come and get us. I have a lot of cheerleading stuff to go over when I get home. We're having practice after school tomorrow."

A few seconds later Miss Hawkins, Miss Carbone, and the two pin-ladies reappeared. They all checked out my breeches and I was given two appointments for fittings the following week, which was also going to be Easter vacation.

It wasn't until we were in the car and nearly home

that I realized there was something odd about the Blair & Harper bridal show.

"Listen," I said, turning to Monique, "where's the groom?"

"The who?"

"The groom. The person the bride marries. And the . . . the best man. And the bride's father. Don't they have any men at all in the bridal show?"

"Oh, men," Monique said. "Oh, sure they do. The bride has to come down the aisle on her father's arm. They'll be walking right behind you. And then when you get to the altar, the best man and the groom will be standing there and the best man will take the ring off the cushion to give to the groom to put on the bride's finger."

"So where are they?"

"Who?"

"The men." I could tell Monique's mind was back on her cheerleading.

"Oh, don't worry. They'll be there. At the final rehearsal. The model agency sends them."

"Oh," I nodded. "It's too bad the model agency couldn't send Blair & Harper a ring-bearer, too."

"Are you still worrying about that? You're crazy. If they sent a real boy to be the ring-bearer then they wouldn't have made you one."

"I know," I sighed. "That's just what I mean."

It was about eight o'clock when I got home and I was hoping to sneak into my room without having to see or talk to anyone. I noticed that the door to Dad's study was closed but, to my surprise, Mom was in the kitchen. And she appeared to be cooking up a storm. She even had on an apron and she was cutting up stew vegetables and chunks of beef.

"Hi!" she called out cheerily, just like any other mother.

I went on into the kitchen and peered into the big cooking pot on the stove. Chopped onions were sizzling merrily in some yellow fat in the bottom of the pot. Even with the exhaust fan going, you could smell them.

"What's all this?" I asked.

Mom laughed. "Don't act so surprised. You've seen me cook before, Cress. I thought I'd catch up a little, fix a beef stew for the weekend. This *was* supposed to be my week 'on' for meals, you know."

"I know," I said glumly. Dad had been carrying on bravely for a week and a half now because of Mom's trip to Minneapolis. Now the whole schedule would have to be revised because Mom owed Dad three cooking days. The week always began with Monday for our household-chore assignments.

"Well," Mom said brightly, "how did it go this evening? Did you have your fitting?"

"Oh yes. And we had a rehearsal, too." So far I hadn't told a single lie.

Mom began taking down a few small jars from the herb shelf.

"And what about you?" I asked quickly, anxious to get off the subject of the bridal show.

She turned around startled, smiling. "Me?"

"Yes. Your trip to Minneapolis. You didn't have a chance to tell me much about it."

I could see she was pleased I was asking. "Do you really want to know?"

"Yes, of course I do." I sat down at the big round wooden kitchen table and reached for a banana from the stainless steel fruit bowl in the center.

"Oh, good," she said. "I'm glad you're interested. I won't bore you with the details. But the meeting had to do with passing equal-rights laws. That means that no one should be discriminated against by law because of sex, whether the law has to do with drafting people into the army or with giving a working parent a temporary leave of absence from their job to take care of a new baby at home."

I began to peel the banana slowly. "You mean that women . . . girls . . . would be drafted into the army, and that men would get to stay at home to feed and burp the baby until it got older?"

"Exactly."

I bit off the tip of the banana. "I don't know if

it's such a good idea, though. I wouldn't want to be drafted. I don't think I'd like being in the army and I certainly wouldn't like to go fight in a war."

"Do you think all men like the idea of being drafted and fighting in wars, Cress?"

"Well then, why don't they do it the other way around and liberate men from going in the army?"

"A good suggestion. Because men really need to be liberated, too. It's a complex and interesting question." Mom wiped her hands on her apron. "Cress, I've got an idea. You really should hear all the sides, and these meetings and discussions I've been attending are very stimulating. The next trip I go on, I'd like to take you along with me!"

I looked up, startled. "Even if it's in the middle of school?"

"Even if it's in the middle of school. You'd learn more at one of our women's rights sessions than you would in a whole month of school. And it would have a lot more bearing on your future."

What an idea! I could just see myself telling Monique and the other kids at school that I'd be going away for a week to a women's liberation conference with my mother.

I polished off the rest of the banana. "If it's really all right to miss school," I said, talking with my mouth still full, "do you know where I'd really like to go?"

117

Mom was browning the chunks of meat in the stewpot. She turned around expectantly. "Where?"

"To Arizona," I said. "The second week in June. For Xandra's wedding!"

Mom's smile faded. "Oh, so you know all about that," she said without much interest. "Well, I don't think you'd find that nearly as stimulating. And, by the way, I had a letter from your Aunt Helen the other day." Aunt Helen was Xandra's mother and my mother's older sister. "She's not exactly overjoyed at what Xandra's doing either."

"Why not?"

"Well, for different reasons from mine, of course. Helen believes that getting married is the greatest thing that Xandra could do. And she's always said college is the best place for a girl to catch a husband. But she was hoping Xandra would get a husband who could step right into a really good job or who came from a rich family. Also, she wanted Xandra to get her degree first because, to Helen's mind, a degree is such a nice decoration for a woman to have."

I kicked at the table leg. "Everyone's picking on Xandra terribly," I said. "I guess you know that you made her feel awful. You made me feel awful, too. I didn't even tell you, but I spoke to Xandra on the telephone while you were away. She isn't coming

 118

here for Easter and she isn't coming . . . any other time either. I don't think she would feel . . . well . . . comfortable here anymore."

"Oh, nonsense, Cress," Mom said a little impatiently. "You're making too big an issue of it."

"I am not! Don't you understand that I really love Xandra? And now I'm going to miss her so much. And I can't even go to the wedding. And after that I'll never see her again."

Mom jabbed the wooden spoon into the stewpot and began poking at the chunks of browning meat.

"You're being ridiculously emotional about all this, Cress. You're blaming me for something foolish Xandra is doing, simply because I spoke my mind about it."

I got up and made for the kitchen doorway. "But *I* don't happen to think Xandra's doing something foolish. I think she's doing a beautiful thing. And I think that *your* ideas are crazy. Girls being drafted, men staying home to take care of babies or to do the housework and cooking while their wives go to medical school to become doctors! It's all so . . . *stupid!*"

Mom looked up at me with her lips pressed together in a tight smile. She didn't say a word.

"And I'll tell you one more thing," I said, my voice getting louder and shriller. "I'm going to give

119

Xandra a beautiful wedding present. And nobody's going to stop me. I'm going to make it myself, too. In metal-sculpture club at school."

Mom opened her mouth as though she was about to speak. But I kept right on ranting.

"So don't even think of my going on a trip with you to one of your meetings. Because the club meets on Friday afternoons after school and whatever happens I'm not missing school on Fridays between now and the end of the term!"

I stormed down the hallway to my room. As I passed Dad's study, the door opened a crack and he popped his head out like a jack-in-the-box with a slightly worried grin.

"Everything under control out here?"

"Everything's perfectly healthy and normal," Mom called out to him from the kitchen. "I'm being me and Cress is being Cress. And that's the way things are around here lately."

As usual, I couldn't tell if she was being serious or sarcastic. If my mother really liked me having my own opinions, why did I always feel she was trying to force *her* opinions on me?

10

The crazy April weather had changed. Next morning was stormy, cold, and windy, with an icy rain falling. Dressed in a hooded ski jacket, long yellow slicker, and black rain boots, I made my way down to Monique's place carrying my books in a zippered plastic bag.

I had promised Monique the night before that I would call for her in the morning because she had so many things to carry to school besides her books—two drum majorette costumes, three twirling batons, and an extra pair of white boots.

The Patten household was in an early morning uproar. Geraldine opened the door, glowering.

"Look here, now," she said, "I'm not driving anybody anywhere this filthy morning. These people want a chauffeur, let them hire one. Not me."

"But the reason I'm calling for Monique," I protested innocently, "is we're *supposed* to go to school on the bus."

121

"Oh," she said, sounding almost disappointed. "Come on in, then. They all overslept. Everybody's in a bad mood so don't say I didn't warn you."

I wandered into the breakfast room. Monique, her usually silken-smooth hair hanging in pale shreds around her face, was standing over the breakfast table, half-dressed, stuffing a hot cross bun into her mouth.

"Of course *you're* on time," she said irritably. "We all stayed up so late packing last night."

"Packing? Why? Are you going somewhere?"

Monique nodded, taking a sip of orange juice. "Last minute," she mumbled. "Barbados. Leaving tonight. With my mother."

"What for?"

Monique swallowed her mouthful. "Vacation, silly. Well, also there *is* going to be some fashion modeling at the hotel and they can probably use me. You know, Easter is very big in the islands."

I nodded. "So you'll be gone all of Easter vacation."

"Mmmm. My Dad'll probably join us for the next weekend. Perfect timing, don't you think?"

"But what about Blair & Harper?" I asked with a worried frown.

"What about them?"

"I have two costume fittings next week."

"That's right," Monique agreed. "*You* have two

costume fittings. But my dress is all fitted and I'll be back in time for the evening dress rehearsal a week from Monday."

How stupid of me. I'd just gone along thinking Monique would be coming with me to my fittings and that Geraldine would drive us. "So how'm I supposed to get to Blair & Harper?" I asked lamely. "It's a good long way."

Monique shrugged. "Get your mother to drive you."

"No, thank you!" I said fiercely. "What a dumb idea."

"So go on your bike," Monique murmured, trailing off toward the stairs to finish getting ready for school. "It's far. But think of all the weight you'll lose."

I stuck my hands on my hips. "You don't have to get nasty," I snapped, my cheeks getting fiery.

"Oh, come on," Monique said, leaning over the bannister. "I was only kidding, Cress. Can't you take a joke?"

Monique took so long getting ready (while I waited downstairs wishing I'd never let her see me in those rose-colored tights) that we were late for the school bus and Mrs. Patten herself had to drive us to school.

"Don't forget. Come and watch me at cheerleading practice in the gym at 3:15," Monique called

123

out as we separated for classes in the main corridor of the school.

"Can't," I called back over my shoulder. "I've got metal-sculpture club today at 3:15."

I peered down at my big notebook to see if the sketch of the museum owl I wanted to make for Xandra was still sitting in its cardboard folder between the pages. It was.

Even though I hadn't heard anything all week from Mr. Grinnell, I didn't see how the club could be so crowded that there wouldn't be room in it for me. I'd signed up very early. And I was looking forward to starting work on Xandra's wedding present that very afternoon.

As soon as the three o'clock gong sounded, I hurried down to the metal-shop room on the second floor. To my surprise the door was open but the room was completely empty. I was probably too early.

I began to wander around the room examining the different machines for pressing, stamping, and cutting metal, and the tools for beating and hammering that I'd be using to pound and shape the body and wings of the owl. Then I picked up a small piece of coppery-colored metal that was lying on one of the workbenches. It was just the right thinness and size for an owl's wing, except of course it would need to have the pattern of individual feathers worked onto the face of it.

"Don't touch anything in this room," a deep voice said directly behind me. I dropped the piece of metal with a start and it landed on the workbench with a puny clank. I knew that voice. And I hated it.

Sure enough, when I turned around there stood Roger Hollister.

"How'd you get in here, anyhow?" he asked suspiciously.

I was so upset at the very sight of Roger that I was already beginning to shake with rage. "Through the door, of course, it was wide open. Anything wrong with that?"

Roger drew a heavy bunch of keys from his pocket and waved them under my nose importantly. "Yeah. It was supposed to be locked."

"Well, whose fault is that?" I snapped at Roger, brushing past him. "If you're the caretaker around here why don't you do your job right? Anyhow, what's the difference if it was open? Metal-sculpture club is supposed to meet here in a few minutes."

Roger's mouth curled into an unpleasant grin. "Yeah, well, sorry to disappoint you, kid. But it won't."

"It won't? The club isn't meeting? Why not?"

"Because it's called off for today. Don't you know

anything that goes on around here? Mr. Grinnell's out of school since Wednesday. He slipped and fell at home. Hurt his back. Now, if you were a fella, and you were in one of Mr. Grinnell's regular shop classes, you'd know all about it. But being you're not. . . ."

"Okay," I said, cutting Roger short. "So what? So I'm not a fella. And I'm finding out about it now. When is Mr. Grinnell coming back to school? Will there be a club meeting next week?"

Roger sneered. "Next week's Easter vacation."

"I know that. I mean the week after, when school opens."

Roger shrugged. "Don't know. No telling what'll happen. If you're so anxious to sign up for a club, why don't you go down the hall to the cooking room. They got a cooking club, art needlework club, nurse's aid club, all kinds of clubs. What do you want to push yourself in here for?"

"I am *not* pushing myself," I said hotly.

" 'Course you are. You're the biggest little pusher I ever saw. Always wheedling your way into places. Last week out at the lake. Now into the club. Why don't you stop wasting your time? Mr. Grinnell doesn't want any girls in the club. . . ."

"Oh, really!" I was seething openly at Roger now, despising his cold yellow-flecked eyes, the mean twist of his mouth, those sparse revolting hairs on his upper lip. "Well, let me tell you something, Roger

Hollister. If Mr. Grinnell doesn't want me in the club because I'm a girl, then he'll have to tell me so himself. I'll come around again two weeks from today. And if you see Mr. Grinnell in the meantime, you can just tell him what I said!"

For an answer Roger swung the bunch of keys in a furious arc in front of my face, just grazing the tip of my nose. "I'm not taking orders from no girl," he hissed. "Now get yourself outa here, right now!" He bounded toward the doorway. "Out!" he repeated, standing rigidly beside the open door of the metal-shop room.

Walking as slowly, and as tall and straight as I could, I marched past Roger and out into the hall. It took courage because I had the distinct feeling that if I took a split second too long, Roger would let go completely and punch me. He was bigger than I was and stronger, and I could only hate him even more for having those advantages over me.

I did pass the homemaking room as I went down the corridor toward the exit stairs. The door was open and the girls in the cooking club were sitting around deciding what kinds of cookies they would bake that afternoon. I walked on. I already knew how to bake almost any kind of cookie there was. What I wanted to do now was to make a sculptured metal owl to give Xandra as a wedding present. Why would anybody close a door on me for that?

11

School had ended for Easter vacation on a sour note all right. And Easter week wasn't much better. Monique, of course, had gone off to Barbados to model fashions in the sun alongside some tropical swimming pool. She'd come back with one of those luscious rosy-apricot tans, looking dreamier than ever. Davey, I wasn't talking to anymore. Mom was suddenly on a housecleaning and cooking-for-the-freezer kick which I found very peculiar. I was wondering if she was feeling guilty about her arguments with me and Xandra. But when she and I did talk to one another, she sounded just as cool and self-assured as ever.

Mom had hired a team of men to do the spring cleaning and she sort of worked along with them. She always tried to have a man come to do the regular-twice-a-week housecleaning, too, rather than a woman. She said it was "discriminatory" against men to always hire a female cleaning person. Because, of course, Mom believed that jobs should not be assigned on the basis of sex.

I guess the best thing about Easter vacation for me turned out to be the fittings at Blair & Harper after all. Getting there and back on my bike was practically an all-day operation. But I didn't mind because it kept me occupied and at the same time it gave me lots of time to think.

The ring-bearer costume was still awful, of course. But Miss Hawkins and Miss Carbone seemed to like it a lot. They even called in a tall distinguished gray-haired lady who was a vice-president at Blair & Harper to see it on me.

The first fitting was on Tuesday morning at eleven and the second one on Thursday morning. By the second fitting, my costume was all finished including the little white satin pillow on which the ring would be resting when I walked down the aisle.

Miss Hawkins wanted me to do a "measured walk" and she showed me how to take a slight pause, to the count of two, each time I put a foot forward, and also how not to lose my balance while taking such slow steps.

"Here now," she instructed, taking off one of the huge rings she wore and placing it in the center of the cushion. The ring had a chunky yellow stone in the center, like an oversized cat's eye.

"Now walk," Miss Hawkins said. I marched down the length of the narrow carpeted corridor between the two rows of dressing rooms while Miss Hawkins, a short distance behind, hummed the wedding march in a cracked contralto.

I came to the end and turned around, relieved but worried. "I don't know," I said. "The ring didn't fall off the cushion but it wobbled an awful lot."

"Clara!" Miss Hawkins commanded without another word to me. Miss Carbone, who had remained behind at the dressing room entrance, arms crossed and smiling in admiration, came rushing over.

"Yes?" she asked anxiously.

"See to it that the wedding band is secured to the cushion somehow. But not so tightly that the best man can't get it off. A long, pearl-headed pin thrust into the cushion at a sharp angle ought to do the trick."

"Right," Miss Carbone said amiably. "Will do."

"Well, that's it for *you*," Miss Hawkins said to me almost cheerily. "Your costume is truly elegant and if you do everything just as I've told you, you could even be the hit of our show." She turned to Miss Carbone. "This could actually revive the ring-bearer tradition in formal weddings. And it makes for a nice bit of extra custom design and sewing, if you know what I mean."

Miss Carbone nodded and Miss Hawkins propelled me back toward the dressing room. I couldn't tell if her hand on the back of my neck was meant to guide me in a kindly way or to push me so that I'd be sure to get where I was going.

I got back into my bicycling jeans and denim jacket and took the escalator down to the main floor. The next rehearsal would be on Monday evening when Monique got back, and the first "performance" of the Blair & Harper bridal show would be on the following Thursday evening in 'The Pecan Tree' restaurant.

The main floor was crawling with people. Kids were home from school and college, and everybody was shopping for spring and summer clothes and all sorts of other things. I was pretty hungry because I hadn't eaten anything since breakfast, so I just naturally eased my way over to the Gourmet Pantry department in the northwest corner of the store. Occasionally they gave out free samples of things to taste. On Tuesday, for instance, they had put out a whole Danish salami cut into thin slices. There were free crackers, too, and I ate so many pieces of salami on crackers that I wasn't even hungry enough to buy the hamburger I'd planned to have for lunch before starting back for home. The salami was pretty tasty, too.

This time, there was a china-doll blonde lady standing beside the free-sample table and smearing

131

bits of some new kind of cheese spread onto very thin wafer-crackers. I took one and walked away among the displays of pickled peaches and fancy imported jams to eat it. The cheese was nice and creamy but it was awfully garlicky. No salami anywhere. I decided to go back for one more cracker with cheese and then go get a hamburger and a chocolate shake at the hamburger stand in the shopping center.

The china doll lit up when she saw me again. She handed me a cracker with an extra-large amount of cheese spread on it and said, "Ah, you liked that." She held up one of the little packets of cheese from France. "Only $1.59 for a 4-ounce package," she said professionally. "Makes a very nice gift and it'll keep 'til Mother's Day." Her eyes swept past me to another possible customer and she swiftly smeared another cracker and handed it to someone over my shoulder. "How about you? Would *you* like to try one, young man?"

I turned around in idle curiosity. A beet-red face and a pair of shocked eyes met my glance. It was Davey Link!

He was standing there helplessly, a broken cracker in his right hand, and creamy white cheese smeared across three fingers. The blonde cheese-lady thrust a tiny paper napkin at him. "Please do move along, children, so that others may sample our product."

Davey looked so confused and he was blushing so hard that I led him away to the corner where the shelves of jams and pickled peaches were.

"Here," I said, "give me that and you take mine." I carefully lifted the two pieces of broken cracker out of Davey's hand and wiped the cheese off his fingers with the paper napkin. Then I put my cheese-heaped cracker in his hand.

"But this one's yours, Cress."

"That's okay," I said. "The cheese tastes too garlicky for me. Maybe you'll like it."

Davey popped the whole thing into his mouth at once and gulped it down. "I like it," he said, with a more relaxed expression on his face. Then, "Gee, I was so surprised to bump into you, Cress."

"What are you doing here, anyway, Davey?"

"Oh, just killing a little time. I was walking around the store and I saw the lady giving out samples. How about you?"

"Well, the same for me. . . ."

"Say," Davey gasped, as if he'd only just remembered, "isn't this the place that was having that fashion show you were going to be in? Did they have it yet or when is it?"

"It's not for a couple of weeks yet," I said, purposely vague. I knew I'd have to get away from Davey before he asked me too many more questions and I had to lie about still being a flower girl in the

133

bridal show. "Well, it was nice seeing you, Davey, but I think I have to be going now," I said, feeling awkward.

"I'm thirsty from that cheese," Davey remarked. "Do you happen to know if they're giving out any free drinks?"

"I don't think so," I said. "But you could ask someone where there's a water fountain."

We began to stroll aimlessly through the crowd, away from the Gourmet Pantry. Davey seemed embarrassed again. "Say, did you ever get that package I sent you, Cress?"

I nodded.

"And there was a letter in it."

"I know. Thanks for . . . for wishing me luck in the bridal show."

It was Davey's turn to nod. "Oh, and by the way, some things have happened since I wrote you that letter."

I turned. "What things?"

"Well, I signed up to go to a naval camp this summer. They've got a 65-foot flagship and a fleet of about 50 boats. Well, actually, it's more of a sailing camp. But I can really consider it the start of my naval career. Two months sooner than I expected, Camp begins the first of July."

"Very good," I said, adding with a bitterness that surprised even me. "And I'm sure they won't have

 134

any leaky old rowboats *there,* will they?"

Davey looked startled for a moment but I could tell he knew what I was referring to. "Oh, gee, that reminds me," he said, "I told Rodge I'd probably meet him up at the lake this afternoon."

The mention of Roger's name really made me see red. "So you and he are still good friends?"

Davey looked puzzled. "Well, yes. By the way, I wrote you in the letter about what happened to those Cokes, didn't I? How we didn't have anything to drink at the picnic?"

"Yes, you wrote me," I said, tight-lipped. "Did you ever find them?"

"Nah, how could we?"

"Too bad," I said, in a perfectly flat voice. I was looking for a way to get away from Davey quickly now. But he seemed to want to hang on.

"By the way, Cress," Davey said, clearing his throat as though a piece of cracker had gotten stuck in it, "I've been meaning to ask you. Do you still bake cookies after school?"

I stared at Davey, surprised he'd have the nerve to ask.

"Not much," I said.

"I really think your cookies are the greatest," Davey went on, just as though nothing had changed. "They always have an especially good taste to them. And when you put in chocolate chips you really put in a lot. The only kind you ever made that I didn't like were the ones with raisins in them. And the coconut. Like I told you, I never. . . ."

"I never bake cookies anymore, Davey," I broke in. "Never. I'm much too busy for stuff like that."

Davey murmured something that sounded like "too bad," but I couldn't be sure.

"Well, you have a real good time this summer, Davey," I sang out in a bright, sort of artificial voice. And with that, I abruptly veered off into the crowd.

I didn't look back until I got to the north exit of the store where the bicycle parking racks were. By that time, of course, Davey had vanished completely into the crush of shoppers and there was no sign of him anywhere.

12

I stood with my eyes fixed on the neat, petite, look-alike backs of Annette and Marie Pellegrino. Their skinny, fine-boned shoulders were draped in organdy frills. They both wore identical little gold lockets. I could see the fine gold chains glittering on the backs of their necks. Their short, feathery black hair had been cut and arranged so that the two sisters could easily have exchanged heads and, from the back, nobody would have known the difference.

We had about six minutes to go before we marched through the doors and into 'The Pecan Tree' for the Thursday evening first showing of the Blair & Harper bridal show. I was much more nervous than I'd ever expected to be. I was so nervous, in fact, that I wasn't even feeling self-conscious anymore about my frightful rose-colored breeches, super-ruffled shirt, shiny white stockings, or clunky black patent leather shoes—or even about the way the make-up team had snipped and curled my hair into a million ringlets all around my head or reddened my cheeks with greasy blusher.

Directly behind me stood the bride and her "father." All of the men who had been sent by the model agency to participate in the bridal show reminded me of department store dummies. They were tall, with lean legs, arrogant shoulders, and handsome cleancut faces that I think were supposed to show "character." The male models all seemed to be about the same age, too, even the bride's father, except for his hair which was gray at the temples and over the ears. Or maybe it was only made up to look that way.

In fact, I could hear the "father" and the bride talking to each other right behind me. And I could swear he was asking her for a date! So I just couldn't help turning around once or twice. After the second time I stole a glance at them, I heard the father say to the bride, "He's a cute kid, all right."

"Sssh," the bride whispered back. "It's not a 'he.' It's a girl who hasn't exactly got it made in the female charms department."

This was followed by a suppressed chuckle from the bride's father, and my cheeks grew so fiery under my blusher that I was sure the deep rose-red make-up must have turned pale alongside my natural color. On top of that, my head was throbbing, I was sweating all over, and I was beginning to wonder if it was

 138

possible I was going to fall down on the floor soon in a dead faint.

At the very last minute, Miss Hawkins had insisted that I should wear short white gloves, and somebody was sent down to the glove department on the main floor to get a pair. The gloves were making me feel hotter. But at least they were keeping my sweaty palms from drenching the little white satin pillow I carried.

The bride's wedding ring was resting on top of the cushion, fastened down by a pearl-headed pin, like the type used to pin flower corsages onto people's clothing. The ring was one of those very wide gold bands (from the Blair & Harper jewelry department, of course) with an openwork pattern of tiny diamond-shaped cutouts circling around its middle, so it had been easy to stick the corsage pin through one of the openings and into the thick cushion.

Miss Hawkins whipped past the line of the procession, brushing by me on my right side. She was wearing lots of heavy, clanking gold jewelry and her dark-red hair was piled so enormously high on her head and into so many coils and twists that I realized she had to be wearing a wig. Her sharply outlined eyes seemed to dart everywhere at once. After she passed, a jet trail of some venomously strong perfume hung in the air. There were only two minutes to go.

In front of me Marie Pellegrino, on the right, was bending over, examining something on the long billowy skirt of her organdy flower-girl's dress. I took a step nearer and peered down to see what she was looking at. The long, rope-like garland of white camellias and green smilax that looped Marie's line of four flower-girls together had come undone at her skirt where it was supposed to be attached to the draped swathe at the side. I guess Miss Hawkins' clanking wrist jewelry must have hooked onto the garland as she had passed and pulled the end loose.

Marie handed her flower-girl's bouquet to Annette so she could use both hands to try to fasten the end of the garland back onto her dress. But she couldn't make it stay, and both she and Annette began to look around frantically for help.

Way out in front of us, at the head of the bridal procession, Miss Hawkins was now opening the doors to 'The Pecan Tree' and motioning, by slashing one forefinger across the other, that we had only half a minute to go.

"If you can't put it back where it was," I hissed helpfully to Marie, "just hold the end of the garland in your hand along with your bouquet." I figured that nobody could see both sides of the procession at once, so the people on Marie's side would just think that was the way it was supposed to be.

 140

But meantime Annette had managed to spot Miss Carbone who was doing a last-minute arrangement of the bride's veil, just behind me. "Aunt Clara, pssst," Annette stage-whispered, beginning to jump up and down in a very unladylike way. Miss Carbone dropped the veil and hurried over. Annette's panic-stricken eyes pointed like dark, sorrowful arrows to Marie's dress.

"Oh, my God!" Miss Carbone panted, her glance falling instantly on Marie's disconnected flower garland. "A pin, a pin." Her hand went automatically to her collar-bone where she usually kept a few straight pins jabbed into the underside of the lapel of her smock or blouse. But Miss Carbone, like Miss Hawkins, had gotten all dressed up for the occasion. "Would you believe it?" she agonized softly. "I haven't got a single pin on me."

Already the strains of the wedding march could be heard from inside 'The Pecan Tree' and the beginning of the procession was starting to move forward. As I continued to look nervously ahead of me, my attention was suddenly drawn downward to a swooping hand directly beneath my nose. The hand, belonging to none other than Miss Carbone, landed on top of the white satin ring cushion I was carrying and swiftly plucked out the pearl-headed corsage pin. A moment later Miss Carbone thrust

141

the pin into the loose end of the flower garland and skillfully connected it to the organdy swathe on Marie Pellegrino's dress.

Already Annette and Marie had broken into their measured walk toward the altar, and I, too, had to take my first step. "Good luck!" Miss Carbone whispered brightly to her darling nieces, the Pellegrinos. If it wasn't enough that the Pellegrino sisters had taken my flower-girl job away from me, they had now taken the all-important pin anchoring the wedding band to my ring-bearer's cushion!

As I paused after my first step, for the required count of two, I noticed immediately that the wedding ring was bouncing perilously on the puffy cushion. I had a wild impulse, just as we approached the doorway of 'The Pecan Tree,' to lunge forward and grab my pin back out of Marie's skirt. But it was impossible. I had all I could do to keep my step and to keep the bouncing ring from dancing off the cushion. So instead I took a deep breath and solemnly walked through the doors, up the ramp, and onto the spotlighted, gray-carpeted platform inside 'The Pecan Tree.'

Miss Hawkins had warned us that we were not to look at any individual faces in the audience that would be lining both sides of the exhibit platform. She had explained how professional actors (and, of course, professional models) were trained to "play" to the audience but never to really "see" them.

I was so busy counting steps and watching the bobbing ring on the pillow that I could hardly have spared a glance for the audience anyway. Of course, I could hear them. As the music of the wedding march grew louder and began to build to a crescendo for the entrance of the bride, just behind me, the oohs and aahs and other comments of appreciation grew louder, too. There was the sense of a huge mob out there, hundreds of eyes and a blur of faces, most of them women's, fanning out through the tightly packed rows on either side of the long platform that was supposed to represent the main aisle of a big church or wedding hall.

The bridesmaids at the head of the procession had already come to a stop and taken their places along the sides of the platform. Just a few more steps and the flower-girls in front of me would halt, leaving a center space through which I would walk, just ahead of the bride on her father's arm, to the altar. There, the best man would take the ring from the cushion so he could give it to the groom to slip on the bride's finger at the ceremony. And what a relief that would be!

It was a lucky thing, I kept thinking, that the wedding band was such a heavy one. Each time the ring had bounced—so far—it had fallen back onto the cushion on its rim, so that it sat there like a minia-

143

ture crown until, of course, the next fearful bounce.

In front of me, Marie Pellegrino had hesitated slightly a few times, as she glanced down at her end of the garland, and I had quickly taken a shorter step so as not to bump into her. Now, once again, she took a faltering step. But the garland must still have been fastened to her skirt because she went on with a normal step. And then, all of a sudden, with no warning at all, Marie Pellegrino jerked to a halt, stopping dead in front of me!

In the instant that I looked down at the skirt of her dress to see what had gone wrong, not one but *three* catastrophic things happened.

I saw the loosened end of Marie's garland fall with a soft thud onto the gray carpet of the exhibit platform. I saw the bride's golden wedding ring wink a farewell to me as it went rolling off the white satin cushion directly onto the parquet wooden floor of 'The Pecan Tree' restaurant. And I saw below me, in the very first row of the audience, a too, too terribly familiar woman's face. A face with a pointed nose, a smiling mouth, and straggly brown hair that was slightly streaked with gray and pulled back into a bun!

The next moment my feet had tangled like strands of spaghetti and I was flat on my face on the gray carpet of the exhibit platform, the useless white pillow still clutched in my white-gloved hands.

Laughter was all around me like a roaring sea. I tried to scramble to my feet in the tight rose-colored breeches and the laughter seemed to grow even louder. Minutes seemed to drag by, although I suppose they were really only seconds. The bridal procession seemed to surge forward, to press on me from all sides, even to raise me up. . . .

At last I was back on my feet, and the bride, directly behind me, was poking a sharp finger into my back just between my shoulder blades.

"Now walk," she commanded, tight-lipped and quiet-voiced as a gunman. "To the altar. And fast."

I did exactly as she ordered. The laughter seemed to have died a little but it kept coming back in waves, interspersed with buzzes and whispers. I heard one woman say to her friend, "Was that *supposed* to happen, do you think?" Her friend, who had a deep matronly voice, said, "No, of course not. Didn't you see how that page boy went and tripped over the flower-girl just in front of him. Putting a clumsy little kid like him into a wedding procession. You've got to be crazy."

The best man stood at the altar watching my approach with an amused but restrained look on his face. The groom was standing directly in front of him, waiting of course for the bride. Naturally I had no ring on the pillow to offer the best man. But I held it up as I'd been told to anyway.

145

In a barely noticeable gesture, the best man touched my elbow and aimed my glance toward the flower-decked altar. Just beyond it I could see a shadowy figure with a mountain of piled and twisted hair on its head. The figure beckoned and, like a sleepwalker, I went directly through the bowered altar and down the steps behind it, at the far end of the exhibit platform, to where the figure waited. I was immediately collared and hustled through the dim rear of 'The Pecan Tree,' past a screened partition, and through a pair of swinging doors.

In the harsh glare of the restaurant kitchen's fluorescent lights, Miss Hawkins loosened her grip on the back of my neck and glowered down at me. She didn't say a word. Her look said it all.

I decided I had to attack at once. There was no other way. "It wasn't my fault!" I screamed at Cheryl Hawkins. "It was Marie Pellegrino's. She came to a dead stop right in front of me, the stupid idiot! And the reason the ring rolled off the cushion is because Miss Carbone took the pin away from me. To fasten Marie's garland to her skirt. Because it had come loose. It's Miss Carbone's fault. Hers and those two nieces of hers that she's so crazy about. Ask anybody. It's the truth!"

For once, I guess, somebody was telling Miss Hawkins something she didn't already know. Her look changed from one of sheer fury to one of angry surprise. But just as she was opening her mouth to speak, there was a noise and we both looked up in alarm.

The doors from the restaurant had swung open and a woman's figure stepped into the kitchen. I was hoping for it to be Miss Carbone. What fun it would be to see her cringing and apologizing, to watch Miss Hawkins really lash out at her.

But it wasn't Miss Carbone at all. It was my mother.

Mom came toward me smiling, holding up between her right thumb and forefinger a small gleaming object. She began to laugh softly.

"It landed right at my feet," she said to me in amazement. "You couldn't have done a better job if you'd aimed it at me on purpose. Or did you?" The object in Mom's hand, of course, was the wedding ring that had rolled off the satin cushion.

Miss Hawkins came forward. "I'm Cheryl Hawkins," she said, approaching my mother with her hand unmistakably outstretched for the ring. "I'm in charge here."

Mom turned toward Miss Hawkins. "Well then, I suppose this does belong to you," she said, dropping the ring promptly into Miss Hawkins' palm. Miss Hawkins was much taller than Mom, especially with that hairpiece on.

"It doesn't belong to me exactly," Miss Hawkins

corrected Mom, "but to the store, of course. Thank you for bringing it in here, madam. And now if you would please resume your seat. . . ."

Mom gave Miss Hawkins an amused look. "But I didn't really come here to see the fashion show. I actually came to see my daughter, Cress." Mom tilted her chin toward me. "So I've no real interest in going back for the rest of the show."

Miss Hawkins' eyes opened wider and her expression softened noticeably. "Oh, I *see,*" she said, quite cordially. "You're Cress' mother, then. Well, I'm happy to meet you."

Mom nodded politely.

"As you can see," Miss Hawkins went on, "Cress is right here, safe and sound, and no harm done. Her falling down was . . . well, it was just circumstances. Not anybody's fault, really. Not her fault, certainly. In fact, I think the audience may have found it a welcome bit of comic relief. And the only damage done is to Cress' costume." Miss Hawkins turned to me almost kindly. "Would you turn around please, Cress?"

Damage! I turned and looked behind me horrified, as Miss Hawkins hooked a fingernail into the seat of my breeches. I hadn't even thought about the possibility of my breeches bursting.

"Yes, you've split them," Miss Hawkins said mat-

 148

ter-of-factly. "Right down the center. And you've torn some of the fabric, too. However, they can and they will be mended for the two showings on Saturday. So don't worry about that."

Don't worry! My breeches had ripped open down the back in front of everyone. There was white underwear showing through the split all right. Did Miss Hawkins really think I could appear again in front of all those people? Not just the audience (which would at least be different) but the other members of the bridal procession and the Blair & Harper staff people. How many had noticed? How much had they seen?

I went over to my mother and crumpled up in her arms. I never wanted to come *near* the Blair & Harper store again.

"I'm afraid there's something you haven't taken into account," I heard Mom say to Miss Hawkins in a voice that sounded muffled and far away because Mom's arms were wrapped around my head hiding my embarrassment and tears. "And that's the damage to Cress' ego. She's been very humiliated by what's happened. Cress is used to being treated like a person. She's not accustomed to playing the role of court jester."

I didn't hear Miss Hawkins' answer and I couldn't see her face because I just couldn't bear to take my

149

face away from the soft folds of Mom's tan cashmere sweater where I'd buried it. But I did hear the sound of Miss Hawkins' heels clattering away.

A few minutes later somebody from the bridal department came to show us how to get from the kitchen of 'The Pecan Tree' back to the dressing room where I got out of the torn rose-colored breeches and the rest of my costume, put on my regular clothes, and left a message for Monique that I was going home with my mother and not to look for me when Geraldine or Mrs. Patten came to pick us up.

It was wonderful driving home through the dark in the car beside Mom. She didn't say a word, even though there were so many things I still had to explain to her about the bridal show. And there were things, too, that I wanted her to explain to me —mainly, what made her come to the show in the first place.

But none of that seemed to matter just then. I knew Mom's silence wasn't an angry silence. It wasn't even one of her patient and amused silences. It was a warm, understanding silence. And it was just right.

13

"There really isn't any medicine but time for a badly injured ego," Mom said, a couple of hours later, after she and Dad and I had talked calmly and quietly about my entire Blair & Harper experience. "But how about a cup of hot chocolate with a blob of whipped cream on top, anyway?"

Mom brought me the hot chocolate in bed and sat down on the edge while I sipped it. "I'm glad you understood why I made up my mind to come to the bridal show, Cress," Mom said. "You'd been acting so moody lately. And so really . . . well, hostile toward me. I felt your wanting to be in the bridal show was your way of identifying with Xandra and her marriage, and defying me. Well, it wasn't *quite* that. But anyhow, I thought I should go and see what it was all about for you. And then, when I saw you in that ring-bearer's getup. . . . !"

"I know," I said, leaning back against the pillows and laughing.

151

"That's good," Mom said. "You can laugh about it already. You'll be okay."

I nodded. "Tomorrow, when I see Monique at school, I'll tell her to tell them I'm not going to be in the performances on Saturday. They can get somebody else. Or they can do without a ring-bearer in their wedding procession. And if Monique doesn't like it . . . too bad. She never really thinks of anything but herself anyway."

Mom took the empty cup and sort of beamed at me. I could see she was pleased.

"And tomorrow is metal-sculpture club," I added. I was thinking out loud, thinking how I didn't need to be a shining-light flower-girl in Blair & Harper's foolish fashion show because making something with your hands was really much more creative, and what I really wanted to do.

"Metal-sculpture club. That's where you're going to be making the wedding gift for Xandra," Mom said, remembering. "Incidentally," she added, "I think that's a fine idea. Much nicer than buying a present in a store. We'll definitely have to invite Xandra and Bill down here for the presentation before they leave for Ireland."

My heart actually did a flip-flop. These were the first nice words Mom had said about Xandra since their disagreement over Xandra's getting married. But I didn't want to embarrass Mom by letting on

 152

I'd noticed. So I went on quickly and said,

"Provided, of course, Mr. Grinnell, the shop teacher, is back at school. He's been out a lot since he fell and hurt his back a few weeks ago. I sure hope he's there because I've got to get started on that sculpture. So remember, I'll probably be home late tomorrow afternoon."

"Okay," Mom said. "Now just relax and go to sleep."

She tiptoed out and I closed my eyes. It seemed like Mom and I were friends again. We had discussed Monique and we had agreed she was just a "show" friend. Deep down . . . well, there wasn't anything "deep down" about Monique. And although I hadn't said anything to Mom about Davey Link yet, I knew that now I agreed with her about him, too.

And as to Xandra . . . well, possibly Mom was beginning to agree just the tiniest little bit with *me*. So maybe we weren't so far apart after all!

I didn't see Monique until third-period study hall the next morning. She had a funny look on her face when she spotted me. "Are you okay?" she said, looking concerned.

"Sure," I replied, trying to sound blithely indifferent. "I'm fine."

"Oh good," Monique said in a relieved way. "Of

course, I didn't see it happen. I was so far up front in the procession. But naturally we did hear all the . . . um, noise. I'm glad you didn't hurt yourself. Or blame anybody else for making you fall."

"Of course I didn't hurt myself. The carpet was soft. And anyhow, I wasn't that far off the ground to start with. That's one of the advantages of being short. It was just that it was embarrassing, that's all. And being a ring-bearer was a stupid idea to begin with. But of course I do blame someone."

"You do?"

"Sure. That Marie Pellegrino tripped me. Maybe not on purpose. But she did. And the other person whose fault it was is that Miss Carbone. By taking that pin out of my ring cushion, she was definitely disobeying Miss Hawkins' instructions. And I can prove it."

Monique looked worried again. "But you aren't going to press charges, are you?"

"Press *what?*"

"Charges. You know. Like suing Blair & Harper for negligence or anything like that. Because you couldn't anyway. They're covered in case of accidents. You had your father sign a release form when you were hired to be a model in the bridal show. Remember?"

"Oh that," I said, remembering the paper I'd brought home to have signed. "Well, I hope it didn't

 154

say anything on there about me having to do two more shows, Saturday morning and afternoon. Because I'm not, you know."

Monique's worried look changed to one of irritation. "You're not? Well, isn't that just like a friend! I told you once before, Cress Richardson, where you'd drop to on my list if you ever let me down like that after I did you a favor. . . ."

"I know, I know," I cut in, "all about how many other friends you've got who are four feet two. Did it ever cross your mind, Monique, that maybe I did *you* a favor, just by *being* four feet two?"

Monique brushed the question aside. "Well, look, if you're not hurt or anything from falling down, and your costume's being sewed up again, why can't you be in the showings tomorrow?"

"I can't because I won't," I said stubbornly. "And I won't because the whole thing's an insult. I feel like an organ-grinder's monkey in that costume. And now that I did fall down and lose the ring and tear my breeches, the news has gotten around and everyone's going to be watching me, just waiting for me to do some other dumb thing. So I'm staying out of it altogether."

Monique swished her hips in annoyance. "I suppose you think I never dropped a baton while leading a cheer. It happens. What *I* think is you're just sore because you weren't a flower-girl."

155

"If you must know," I retorted, "I think bridal fashion shows are pretty dopey to begin with. People get dressed up and parade around like mechanical dolls to get other people to make big splashy show-off weddings so that businesses that don't serve any really important purpose can make a lot of money."

Monique glanced up at the study hall clock and gathered up her books. "Well, I'm sorry, but it still sounds like a whole lot of sore-loser talk to me." She began to sideskip gracefully along the row of seats to the aisle. "See you around, Cress. Hope you have fun."

"You, too," I called after her, in a dead voice.

I couldn't honestly say whether or not I *would* have felt differently about the bridal show if I'd been a lead flower-girl like Monique, or even a number four flower-girl like I was supposed to have been in the first place. But maybe it was a good thing I'd turned out to be a page boy in a costume I hated. It had helped me to see the Blair & Harper bridal show for what it really was. That and a little conversation with my mother, of course.

In many ways, I dreaded going down to the metal-shop room at 3 o'clock. I was sure the first person I saw would be Roger Hollister. And our whole ugly relationship would spring into action again. I was even beginning to think that maybe my being so

 156

persistent about getting into the metal-sculpture club was just to prove to Roger that I could do it.

To my surprise and relief Roger was nowhere in sight. The door of the shop-room was open, six or seven boys were puttering around among the workbenches, and Mr. Grinnell was sitting at his desk with a newspaper spread out in front of him.

He looked older and tireder than the last time I'd seen him. I guess maybe he'd been having a lot of pain with his back. He looked up at me glumly. "Yes?"

"I'm Cress Richardson," I announced. "I registered for the club a few weeks ago. I guess today's the first meeting, right?" I looked brightly around the room.

Mr. Grinnell scratched his cheek. If he remembered me at all, he didn't give any indication. It crossed my mind that maybe, when he'd taken that fall, he'd had some kind of a head injury that affected his memory.

"You remember me, don't you, from when I signed up?" I asked anxiously.

There was no answer but after a few seconds Mr. Grinnell pushed his desk chair back and stood up, plunging his hands into his trouser pockets and looking down at the floor. He shook his head back and forth a few times. "Sorry, young lady. Club's full up."

157

"But how can it be? There're only six people here."

Mr. Grinnell lifted his head and appeared to be counting the boys in the room. "Seven," he corrected me. "Seven. And a few more coming that are already members. And that's it. Can't take any more than that."

"But when I spoke to you that other time you said you'd take twelve, or maybe even fifteen."

Mr. Grinnell sat down again, still shaking his head. "I haven't been too well. Big strain, these after-school clubs. They don't pay you a penny more for doing it, you know."

A thought occurred to me. "Did Roger Hollister talk to you about me, by any chance? I know he's around the shop-room a lot. Last time I was here, when you were out sick, he was even in charge of the keys."

Mr. Grinnell's look sharpened. "Recommendations won't help a bit, missy. I've already told you the club's closed."

I nearly laughed. The idea of Roger Hollister recommending *me* for anything. I was beginning to realize though, that, mean as he was, Roger probably hadn't influenced Mr. Grinnell with his prejudices. He didn't need to because Mr. Grinnell had his own.

I decided to come right to the point. "If the real

reason you won't take me in the club," I said boldly, "is because I'm a girl, then I'd like you to come right out and say it. Because I *did* sign up early, and I *wouldn't* be much trouble—I only need a *little* help—and I can't think of any other good reason for keeping me out."

Mr. Grinnell suddenly spun around in his chair so that the light caught his glasses in a steely flash. "Aha!" he exclaimed, pointing a finger at me. "So you're one of those. I knew there was something behind this. Well, I hope you know, young lady, that there's no room in this department or in this school for troublemakers."

"I don't understand," I said lamely, beginning to grow very uncomfortable. Several of the boys at the workbenches had turned around to stare at me. "Why is it troublemaking to want to join a school club?"

Mr. Grinnell got up from his desk and began to walk toward the door. It was pretty clear that he was showing me the way out. I followed him, thinking how much this scene was beginning to remind me of the last time with Roger Hollister.

When he reached the doorway, Mr. Grinnell folded his arms. He narrowed his eyes and lowered his voice, evidently not wanting the boys inside the shop-room to hear him. "Just giving you fair warning, Little Miss Innocence, that I'm on to your kind.

Stirring up trouble everywhere you go. Next thing you know, it'll be student sit-ins and student strikes, and then a whole student revolution. It only takes a little thing like this to start it. And, of course, somebody who's looking for it."

I was flushed with shock and embarrassment. But I had to try to explain.

"I'd just like to tell you," I said to Mr. Grinnell, my voice quaking because I'd never had any argument like this with a teacher before, "that you're wrong about me. I'm not trying to 'start' anything. I'm not any kind of a troublemaker. I only wanted to make something . . . to give somebody . . . I love . . . who's going to get married . . . and who. . . ."

I raced out the door and down the corridor, unable to finish the sentence, hot tears steaming beneath my eyelids. I think the real reason I was crying was because I was so angry. And because I hadn't told Mr. Grinnell what I really wanted to tell him: that *he* might not want me in his club because I was a girl, but that I didn't want to *be* in his club because he was a prejudiced, narrow-minded, horrible, old man!

I was back at my old game of trying to sneak into the house and get to my room without having to talk

 160

or explain anything to anybody. Even though Mom and I were friends again, my run-in with Mr. Grinnell was less than an hour old, and it was still too raw coming, as it did, right on top of the Blair & Harper disaster.

But Mom was in her study because she'd been doing a lot of work at home that week, and I wasn't in the house five minutes before I'd blurted out the whole story of how it was pretty clear Mr. Grinnell wouldn't let me in the metal-sculpture club because I was a girl.

At first Mom was very comforting, the way she had been about the bridal-show episode. Then she wanted to know a lot more details. Where had I first seen the poster announcing the formation of the club? What exactly had the poster said? When had I registered for the club? What had Mr. Grinnell's words to me been at that time? Were there any witnesses, either the last time I'd spoken to Mr. Grinnell or this time?

Then Mom sat down at her desk and began writing all my answers down on a long, legal-size pad of ruled yellow paper in a mixture of shorthand and longhand. She looked as though she was back at her old job as a case-worker in the social service agency. As for me, I felt like a witness to a murder being grilled by one of those big-time super-sleuth lawyers.

After a while, Mom did more and more writing and less and less comforting. Finally, really business-like, she said, "Okay. You can go now."

She closed her study door and I went to my room to try to start my term paper for history class. It was a good thing I wasn't going to be in the two big Saturday showings of the Blair & Harper bridal show because I was going to have to spend most of tomorrow in the public library. Another place I wanted to go to was the county museum to find out the price of a reproduction copy of the owl I wanted to give Xandra. Because now it certainly didn't look as though I was going to get to make her one!

Dad got home at about six o'clock and we ate dinner. According to the family job schedule, it was supposed to be my week to fix meals. But because Mom had been away, and then Dad had missed a few evenings on account of business appointments, they were still trying to even out their obligations to one another. So we had one of Mom's cooked meals out of the freezer that evening.

I went to my room after dinner to do some more work on my term paper. Then, about eight o'clock, cars began pulling into the drive and the doorbell started ringing. I could hear the whole house filling up with women's voices.

I opened the door of my room a crack and came face to face with Dad who must have popped out the door of his study at the very same moment. Dad grinned across the hallway at me and said "Hi" in that crinkly-eyed way that made you fall in love with him all over again each time he did it.

I glanced toward the living room. "I didn't know Mom was having a meeting here tonight."

Dad clicked his tongue against the inside of his mouth the way he sometimes did. "She wasn't. Seems something came up at the last minute. Says she'll explain all about it later. Anyhow, how's about you and me going out on the town and having a good old-fashioned evening at the movies, with popcorn and candy bars. And then maybe a chocolate ice cream soda or a hot fudge frappe afterward. What say?"

"Honestly? Are you sure you don't have work to do?"

"I'm sure I *do* have work to do. But who can work in this racket. Let's go!"

Was I happy! It had been a long time since Dad and I had gone out together like that. Somehow I never enjoyed our going out as much when Mom was away on a trip, because at times like that it always seemed like we were just trying to escape an empty house, or that Dad was trying to keep me happy out of a sense of duty.

By the time we left, there were fourteen women in the living room and it was filling up fast. When we

163

got back, at about eleven, the last car was just pulling away. Mom came to the door looking hot and straggly, but smiling triumphantly.

"We had a simply great evening," she announced. "Our committee is set to go." She placed both hands on my shoulders. "And I guarantee you, Cress, that you'll be starting your owl for Xandra on Friday afternoon at the very next meeting of the metal-sculpture club."

I looked up at her in alarm. "You didn't phone Mr. Grinnell or anything like that, did you?"

"Of course not," she assured me. "We don't operate that crudely. What I've done, my dears," she said, addressing both Dad and me with pride, "is organize a committee to check out equal rights and opportunities for all students in the county public schools —all, of course, meaning boys *and* girls. As the problem Cress told me about this afternoon is the most pressing, we'll approach the authorities at her school first thing on Monday morning."

I sat down, cross-legged, on one of the big, thick living room rugs. "But you don't understand," I protested, shaking my head. "I don't *want* to be in the metal-sculpture club anymore. If Mr. Grinnell was forced to take me in . . . well, it just wouldn't be any good. I'd feel self-conscious . . . ashamed. Don't you see?"

Mom got down on her knees beside me, while Dad

went out to the kitchen to get something to drink. She brushed back a lock of hair that had fallen into my eyes. "I'm afraid you're the one who doesn't understand, Cress. This is a very important issue. It's . . . well, it's bigger than both of us . . . if you want to put it that way."

"You mean I have to go into the club now, even if I don't want to?"

"Right! We have to fight for your right to be in the club, and then you have to take your place in the club to demonstrate our victory, and to set a clear precedent."

I pulled away from Mom and scrambled to my feet. "That's stupid," I declared. "You can't *make* me join the club. All the kids at school would laugh at me. Everyone would know how my mother made a big thing out of it. I'd just die of . . . of embarrassment. It would be like falling down in the Blair & Harper bridal show all over again."

"Not at all," Mom said, getting up and lighting a cigarette. As usual, she was getting cooler while I was getting hotter. "The bridal show was a meaningless charade, a circus. This is an important social issue, vital to every woman and girl in our society. There's a world of difference. And I'd be ashamed of you, Cress, if you couldn't recognize it."

"Then *be* ashamed," I struck back, angrily. "I don't want to be used as an example by your committee. You're not thinking for one minute how I would feel. You're just thinking of leading your army to victory, like . . . like . . . Joan of Arc, or somebody!"

Dad came back into the room with a tall glass in his hand. "What's up?"

Dad was kind and sweet and warm. But why didn't he ever get *into* anything? Why was he always playing the innocent bystander? Or was that just his tactful way of always being on Mom's side?

"Do you want to know something?" I shouted at Mom, completely ignoring Dad. "You'd have to carry me kicking and screaming into that club next Friday. And I'd let everybody know you were forcing me. I'd even tell them that *you* put me up to trying to get into the club in the first place because you wanted to start trouble in the school, just like Mr. Grinnell accused *me* of doing. How would you like that!"

Mom didn't answer. Very calmly she stubbed out her cigarette and started putting out lights in the living room. "Okay, Cress," she said at last. "Just relax. If it's too much to ask of you, forget it. But we'll still take the committee's resolution right to the top administration at your school. Your attempts to join the club are now a matter of record, so we can function very well without your personal cooperation."

"But you would still use my name?"

"Of course. We would have to."

I picked up a thick sheaf of Mom's committee notes from one of the tables and slammed them to the floor.

"But I don't *want* you to!" I screamed. "Why can't you understand a single thing I'm saying to you!"

Dad rushed over and put his arms around me in something half way between a bear hug and an arm-lock. "I have a great idea," he said, speaking in a muffled, breathy voice and beginning to shepherd me toward my room. "We'll all go to bed now, calmly and quietly. And we'll talk about all this again in the morning, after a good night's sleep."

"No we *won't,*" I yelled bitterly, letting my voice carry over my shoulder to where my mother was standing stock still in the middle of the living room, looking down in shock at the splash of scattered papers.

"And the reason we won't talk about it in the morning," I continued, much louder and with my voice breaking, "is because I won't *be* here in the morning!"

But nobody seemed to pay the least bit of attention to what I was saying.

The next instant I broke free from Dad, ran into my room, and slammed, locked, and barricaded the door.

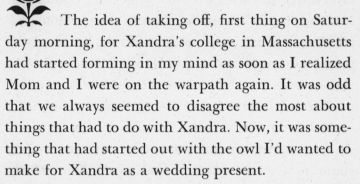

14

The idea of taking off, first thing on Saturday morning, for Xandra's college in Massachusetts had started forming in my mind as soon as I realized Mom and I were on the warpath again. It was odd that we always seemed to disagree the most about things that had to do with Xandra. Now, it was something that had started out with the owl I'd wanted to make for Xandra as a wedding present.

By five A.M. I was wide awake, stealthily getting dressed, and stuffing some extra pants, sweaters, and underwear in a big dirty canvas knapsack I had. I had seventeen dollars in the little green metal safe I kept under my bed, to which only I knew the combination.

With the first crack of the day's light I was out of the house and walking my bike down the gravel path, trying to crunch as softly as possible. It was pretty far to the long-distance bus station in town, and I had no idea when the first bus for central Massachusetts came along. But I knew there was one some time around eight A.M. because I remembered that one time Xandra's car had broken down, and Dad and I had driven her to the bus stop so she would get back to school only a little late for her Monday morning classes.

It was lovely pedaling along that early on a Saturday morning, even though it was still damp and gray and chill out. I wished I were going a lot farther than Massachusetts. Except for Connecticut, it was practically the next state over—hardly any distance at all, even if it was a two- to three-hour bus trip. Now Ireland, where Xandra and Bill were going in June —that was really far. Miles and miles and miles across the stormy Atlantic.

And suddenly I thought how wonderful it would be if they would only take me with them. Why, I could even keep house for them over there, and then maybe Xandra could manage to continue college *and* work, both at the same time. What a solution that would be to all our problems!

The more I thought about going to live with Xandra and Bill in Ireland, the more I liked it. And how lucky that I wouldn't have to learn a foreign language. I already knew what Irish-English sounded like. It was just a matter of getting used to the accent.

My one-way bus ticket cost seven dollars and change, and the bus was due at 7:53 A.M. Aside from the fact that it would have nearly wiped out my cash-

169

on-hand, I was definitely not interested in a round-trip ticket. I'd chained my bike to a rack in the bus station parking lot. In a few days Mom and Dad could come and claim it. With a kind of glum triumph, I reflected that it was all they would have left of me.

The bus came along and it was nearly empty. I took a seat next to the window, the bus started, and I began to munch on the potato chips and chocolate bars I'd bought at the bus station. A regular breakfast at home had, of course, been out of the question.

Soon we were rolling along on a superhighway that looked exactly like the ones back home, even though we were in Connecticut. And even after we crossed the state line into Massachusetts, the countryside didn't look any different, and the roads were just as wide and as modern, and were filled with just as much traffic. Oh sure, here and there there was a cow or a barn or an apple orchard. But it was all so . . . blah. Now, the Irish countryside, I told myself. That would be really different!

I wasn't aware of feeling nervous until the bus driver called out the name of the town where Xandra's college was. It was the next stop.

How in the world was I going to find Xandra, even though I knew the name of her dormitory and her room number? Already we had driven past part of the college campus on our way into the town, and

 170

there must have been about fifty red brick buildings in sight, large and small, tall and short, but all looking very much the same.

Luckily the town itself turned out to be very small, and the bus stopped just across from the village green. It was exactly like the village greens I'd always read about and seen pictures of in history books about the New England states.

There was something called an Information Center on the green, so as soon as I got off the bus I lugged my knapsack and me directly over there, even though I was feeling dizzy and slightly sick to my stomach. I guess potato chips and candy bars first thing in the morning aren't the greatest. Milk and doughnuts at the bus station would have been a lot better.

The man in the information booth reminded me of Mr. Grinnell except he was dressed in something that looked like a policeman's uniform, or maybe it was just a guard's uniform. I told him the name of the college dormitory I was looking for.

He stared back at me very sternly and took down a sheet of paper from one of the shelves inside the booth. It had a detailed map of the college campus on it, with a key to the names of all the buildings.

"Kind of young for college, aren't you?" he said, with a suspicious air. I wasn't sure if he was serious or not.

171

"Oh, I'm just visiting my sister," I said. I thought 'sister' sounded better than 'cousin.' "She's expecting me," I added.

"Well, you're lucky," he said, holding the map in front of me and pointing at it with the eraser end of a stub of pencil. "The dormitory you're looking for is just here. Not a long walk at all once you get inside the gate. That's about a quarter of a mile from here, just down this road. Now, if it was to be one of those new dorms over on the west campus, you'd need a ride. You sure would. Place keeps growing like an octopus. Tentacles everywhere. College'll be overrunning the town soon. Yep, everybody wants to get educated these days. Everybody."

I nodded because he seemed to want somebody to agree with him. Then I thanked him and lifted my knapsack onto my shoulder, trying not to take my eyes off the map so I wouldn't lose sight of my goal.

Once I got through the main entrance gate to the college, I realized it wasn't going to be too difficult because the buildings were all marked with their names matching the key on the map, and pretty soon I came to Xandra's dormitory. There weren't many people around outside and those that were didn't seem to take any notice of me. Which was just as well. Maybe they thought I was one of those child geniuses that are getting pretty common on college campuses these days. Or maybe they figured me for a dwarf student.

Xandra's room was on the second floor of the three-story building, so I took the stairs up.

Girls were chasing around the corridors half-dressed and there was the sound of showers running. Most of the room doors were open and the girls inside all seemed to be eating or drinking coffee or washing their hair, or all three. Just outside the door to Xandra's room, which was shut, I nearly bumped head on into a girl in dungarees and a brassiere, with a huge bright-green Turkish towel wrapped around her head.

She brushed past me and I knocked timidly on Xandra's door. There was no answer. The girl with the towel on her head turned. "Looking for Xandra?"

I nodded.

"Go on in," she said. "She's in there. I'm her roommate." She disappeared into one of the rooms with an open door.

I turned the knob and walked in. It was a small room just like the others I'd passed, with upper and lower bunk beds against one wall and two study desks against the opposite wall. Xandra had her head in the sink. She was washing her hair, too.

I stood there, hesitating. I didn't want to scare her.

173

But she must have heard me because she lifted her dark shining-wet hair up out of the sink with a whoosh, scattering large drops of water all over the floor. Then her eyes opened wider and she let out a little scream.

I smiled sheepishly and helped her grab onto the towel she was reaching for. She quickly wound it around her head into an immense turban, like her roommate's, and plopped down onto the lower bunk bed, fluttering her fingers against her chest to show me how fast her heart was beating.

"I guess you're surprised to see me," I said, still feeling a little sick to my stomach, and beginning to feel ill-at-ease as well.

"Surprised!" Xandra gasped. "That's hardly the word, Cress." Her eyes narrowed. "Is everything okay? How did you get here?"

"On the bus," I said, preferring to answer the second question and ignore the first one. I sat down in one of the desk chairs opposite Xandra.

"How come Aunt M or Uncle Phil didn't drive you up?"

Xandra sure knew how to get right to the bottom of things. Anyhow, my canvas knapsack was sitting right there beside me on the floor. Before I could answer, she said, "They don't know you're here. You ran away. Right?"

"Xandra, please," I begged, jumping up and put-

 174

ting my arms around her. I was nearly in tears. "Please listen to me. Please don't do anything. I have so many things to explain to you. And I don't feel . . . so good. . . ."

"I thought so," Xandra said, holding me a little bit away from her so she could get a good look at me. "You looked greenish when you came in here. Is there something I can get you?"

"I don't know," I said. "A Coke maybe." Coca-Cola syrup was supposed to be good for settling an upset stomach. Even doctors recommended it. Xandra got up. "Stay here," she said. "I'll be right back."

She was back in a few minutes with an ice cold Coke with lots of ice in it.

"There's a machine at the end of the corridor," she explained. "Now sit down and drink it slowly. You can tell me everything while I'm drying my hair."

An hour and a half later, Xandra's hair was dry, she had listened to my entire saga of woes, and we were on our way to meet Bill at the Student Union building for lunch. Xandra had gone down the hall to phone him shortly after I'd finished drinking my Coke.

"I'm nervous about meeting Bill," I confided, as we started down the steps of the dorm building.

175

"You couldn't be more nervous than I was at Easter time when I had to meet Bill's parents in Wisconsin," Xandra replied.

"Oh, but they must have loved you. Gosh, I'm sorry, Xandra. I've been so busy talking about me, I never even asked you about that."

"They didn't 'love' me," Xandra said dryly. "They were about as opposed to the idea of my marrying Bill as Aunt M was. But for different reasons."

"Oh? Why?"

"Well, they think I'll be a hindrance to Bill, a drawback to his studying and all that. They're afraid I might even have a baby or something. They just don't want Bill to get married until he has his medical degree. And they don't really think my help is worth much to him."

"I see," I said, looking down at the cracks in the pavement where fresh grass and new green weeds were sprouting through. "But that didn't change your minds, yours and Bill's, did it?"

"Not a bit," Xandra said. "But they aren't giving him a penny more than he'll need for tuition and living expenses. So, of course, I'll have to find a job right away. The instant we get there."

Here was a great opening for me. "Xandra," I said, "I have a wonderful idea. I'll come to Ireland with you!" And I told her all about my plan to keep

 176

house for her and Bill so she could both work *and* go to school. "That way . . . well, if things didn't work out . . . uh, that is, between you and Bill . . . you wouldn't be losing anything. Don't you see? You'd still be continuing with college and you could get your degree after all. If you wanted to."

Xandra stopped beneath the branches of a small budding tree. Her face was speckled with shade, now that the sun had come out and the weather had turned breezy.

"Oh, Cress," she said laughing, "you're too much. Judging from that last remark, I'm not at all sure whether you ran away from home or whether Aunt M *sent* you."

My face fell. "It's my own idea, Xandra. Why would it be so impossible for me to go to Ireland with you? I hear stories all the time about teenagers who can't get along at home, and psychologists tell their parents to send them to live with other families for a while. It seems to clear up a lot of their problems."

"You're not a teenager, Cress. You're only eleven."

"I know. But my troubles are starting earlier. Everything is speeded up these days. You know that. Besides, how many mothers are there around like mine? Mothers who would embarrass me so I couldn't even face the kids in my own school anymore?"

177

Xandra smiled and shook her head. I could see she wasn't taking me seriously at all. She hadn't even seemed too terribly sympathetic about my reason for having left home in the first place.

"Whatever you do," Xandra cautioned, as we turned in the path for the Student Union building, "don't mention that wild idea of coming to Ireland with us to Bill. That's all he needs!"

My hopes died. I could understand Bill not wanting me. He didn't even know me. But Xandra not wanting me, refusing to even take my suggestion seriously—that hurt.

Just inside the entrance to the Student Union building, Xandra broke away from me to talk to a stocky, fattish young man with eyeglasses and thinning blonde hair. I stood to one side, waiting for her to finish so we could go on in and meet Bill. The entrance was noisy and crowded, full of students standing around in little groups and reading bulletin-board notices.

After about a minute, Xandra turned and called out to me. "Cress, come on over here."

I trotted over obediently to where she was still standing and talking to the balding, heavy-set young man.

"Cress," she said, turning and gesturing with her hands, "this is Bill. Bill, I'd like you to meet my cousin Cress."

 178

Bill! I gulped. It couldn't be Bill. For one thing, Bill was tall. Taller than this person, and *much* taller than Xandra. Then, of course, Bill didn't have thinning blonde hair. Bill had dark hair and an endearing, charming grin. And Bill didn't wear glasses. Bill, in fact, was so beautiful that any girl, Xandra included, would go to the ends of the earth with him. If this *was* Bill, he was Bill Somebody-Else. He couldn't possibly be the Bill that Xandra was going to marry!

But Bill didn't seem to be the least bit aware that he was the wrong person altogether. He calmly nodded as a sign of acknowledgement at our intro-duction. Then he extended his hand toward me and said crisply, but in a low confidential voice, "Very happy to meet you, Cress. You're the very first mem-ber of Xandra's family that I've met, in fact."

"Now how's that for a famous first?" Xandra re-marked, winking at me.

"Oh, it's nice. I'm very . . . happy . . ." I stam-mered to Bill, "to meet you . . . too."

"Well then," Bill said warmly, "shall we go and get some lunch?"

He put one hand on Xandra's shoulder and one on mine, and propelled us toward the Student Union dining room where we found a table and decided on what to eat. Bill ordered soup and a sandwich, Xandra had a salad and coffee, and I had a ham-

179

burger and a Coke. My stomach was much better but my mind was very unsettled since the shock of meeting Bill.

While we waited for our food, Bill asked me a few polite questions about how long the trip to Massachusetts had taken me and what the weather had been like in New York. One thing I couldn't help noticing about him was that when he asked a question, even an unimportant one, he seemed completely interested in the answer. He kept his eyes so fixed on mine that the lenses of his wire-rimmed glasses never even glinted once. If he knew anything at all about my problems with my mother or my having run away from home, he never said anything about it. I somehow suspected that he did know but was too considerate of my feelings to mention it.

Once I started munching on my hamburger, Bill turned and started talking to Xandra, mostly about some medical-school forms that still had to be filled out. I could see immediately how wrapped up Xandra was in Bill. The more he talked, the less even I seemed to notice his looks. Xandra, I decided, had probably stopped noticing them long ago. The Bill she knew was very different from the Bill I'd been so disappointed in at first glance. And, unlike the groom and the best man and those other handsome cardboard men in the Blair & Harper bridal show, Bill at least was a real person.

 180

But that didn't keep me from getting more and more depressed as I sat there beside Xandra, sopping up the ketchup in my plate with the last of my hamburger bun. Aside from getting a lot of things off my chest (that I now realized Xandra couldn't do a single thing about because she had so many problems of her own), I knew that even though I'd come all the way to Massachusetts, I wasn't *anywhere*.

Having met Bill and watched him and Xandra together, completely involved in their own feelings for each other and in working out their own future, I saw that my idea of going to Ireland with them was crazy, to say the least. What a dope I'd been!

I put my elbows on the table and my chin in my hands, and stared down at the tabletop while Xandra and Bill rattled on. Or rather while Bill talked and Xandra listened, glowing and silent.

Every now and then, just for an instant, Xandra's eyes would swing away from Bill, not toward me but across the room. Was she watching for someone else? Was the tall, dark-haired, good-looking Bill, that I'd originally pictured, going to come through the door of the Student Union dining room? Was all this a mistake? A bad dream? Had I really run away from home in the first place. Or would I soon be waking up in my own bed on an ordinary Saturday morning?

Xandra's eyes began to flash more and more frequently toward the restaurant entrance. Once or twice, even Bill stopped talking for a second and twisted around in his seat to glance toward the doorway.

I maneuvered the straw in my empty Coke glass into my mouth and, with my chin still resting in my hands, began to sip noisily at the dregs of Coke and melting ice. Suddenly Xandra's arm, right beside me, shot up in the air.

I lifted my head and followed the direction of her waving fingers. Hurrying toward our table from the doorway was a medium-tall, dark-haired man in a maroon turtle-neck sweater and light tan trousers. He had brown eyes, a pudgy shapeless nose, and a crooked but beautifully happy grin.

He would have been perfectly acceptable to me, in appearance, as the Bill Xandra *should* have been marrying. But he wasn't a 'Bill' at all. He was, instead, a 'Phil.' And he was already married. To my mother, of course.

Dad plunked himself down with relief at the table, beside Bill and directly opposite me. He leaned slightly forward, his tense, worried eyes meeting mine and fixing themselves there.

"Well, well," he said, "fancy meeting you here!"

 182

15

It was nearly the end of June, and Mom and I were packing my trunk for camp.

Only a couple of hours earlier, Xandra and Bill, married just a week, had stopped by for dinner on their way to New York City. They would be flying away to Ireland the very next day.

I sat on the floor beside the trunk, sewing name tapes on a pile of sweaters.

"Do you think Xandra liked the wedding present I gave her?" I asked Mom.

Mom sat back on her heels. She'd been leaning forward on her knees stuffing blankets and towels into the bottom of the trunk.

"Of course she did. Didn't you see the look of delight on her face when she unwrapped it? And Bill sincerely admired it, too."

It was amazing that Mom and I could even talk about the owl after the trouble it had caused back in April. Of course, the owl I'd given Xandra wasn't the one I had hoped to make for her in the metal-sculpture club. It was a reproduction of a sculptured owl that I had bought at the gift desk in the county museum. And it had cost plenty. In fact, I never would have been able to afford it if not for the money I'd earned from the Blair & Harper fashion show.

So the whole thing was a compromise. But isn't that the way it sometimes is?

Mom made a compromise, too.

You can imagine all the static in the air the day when Dad drove me back home from Xandra's college in Massachusetts. I was angry at Xandra for having phoned Dad and tipped him off to where I was (she'd done that at the same time she'd phoned Bill about meeting for lunch at the Student Union). I was still angry at Bill for turning out to be short and balding (even though he'd turned out to be pretty nice otherwise), I was angry at Dad for sneaking up there to bring me home. And most of all, I was angry at Mom for the same reason I'd run away in the first place.

When Mom and I came face to face it was even worse. We hardly talked at first that weekend, just sort of circled each other stiffly every time we bumped into each other anywhere in the house. And we never talked about the subject of my running away at all.

When we did start to talk, Mom said things like,

 184

"This coming week is supposed to be your week to do the meals. Do you think you can handle it?"

And I said, "Why not? Am I supposed to be sick or something?"

Another time, later on Saturday evening, Mom said, "When are your exams? I'll have to rearrange the schedule so you don't have meal duty that week."

And I said, "What are you worrying about exams for? We only just finished midterms a couple of weeks ago."

Then, on Sunday morning, Mom of all people got into the station wagon to drive me down to the bus station so we could get my bicycle from the rack in the parking lot where I'd chained it. Dad said he had some important papers to go over in his study. Mom and I didn't talk much in the car. But the silence wasn't quite so icy as it had been on Saturday. And one good thing, Mom was perfectly matter-of-fact about hauling the bike into the wagon and bringing it back. No gloating at what a flop my little escapade had been.

And then, late on Sunday afternoon, Mom disappeared into her study for a couple of hours.

When she came out, she announced to Dad and me that she'd had some telephone conferences with members of the committee and they'd decided to take a "more direct" approach toward "school authorities that allowed students to be excluded from

185

certain classes and school clubs on the basis of sex."

Instead of going to *my* school and naming names, Mom said, the committee was going to send a delegation to the school-board meeting later that week.

"At that meeting," Mom said, sounding very serious and businesslike, "we will bring up the issue as a general resolution, but one that is to be strictly enforced starting with the new school year next September."

I thought (and later Dad secretly agreed with me) that the new approach sounded *less* direct than the old one, but I certainly wasn't going to quibble with the language Mom had decided to use. Mom needed to save her pride. And as long as she was going to save me from public embarrassment at the same time . . . well, it seemed we were nearly ready to be friends again.

Maybe on a more lasting basis this time?

The entire spring, starting with April Fools' Day, had been a time of freak weather changes, warm and sunny one minute, then storm-tossed, chill, and rainy the next.

That was the way it was for me, too. My two best friends of nearly a year had turned out to be somehow all wrong for me. I wasn't even too sure anymore that Xandra was doing the right thing in giving up school and marrying Bill with all the problems they were going to have, although I certainly hoped she'd be happy. And my mother—well, I'd found out that she wasn't wrong *all* the time. But she wasn't right all the time, either.

Xandra had told me, what seemed like a very long time ago, that it was very important for me to find out who I was. And Mom had said to me, during one of our clashes early in April, that all she ever wanted me to be was *me*. (And then she'd forgotten all about that and had tried to make me over into *she*.)

Well, here it was the first day of summer and everything, including the weather, was a lot more settled.

In about ten days' time, Davey, Monique, and I would be going off to camp. But not to the same camp. Davey was going to his naval-training camp, and then on to naval prep school in the fall, so I wouldn't be seeing much of him anymore.

Monique was going away to a model-training camp for the summer. There she would learn how to stand and how to walk, how to dress and how to put on makeup like a topnotch, high-salaried fashion model, while studying everything from ballet to baton-twirling on the side. Of course, unlike Davey, Monique would be coming back home after the summer but I knew that by then we would both be looking for different friends.

As for me, I was getting ready to leave for a "wilderness" camp in the Maine woods. For the very first time. It wasn't a camp for girls who wanted to be "girls" or for boys who wanted to be "boys," or even for girls who wanted to be "tomboys." It was a camp for learning survival techniques and how to deal with nature in the raw. From the ground up. And it was for both girls *and* boys.

I was scared silly and already had butterflies in my stomach wondering what kinds of kids I would meet and work with up there—and if I'd even be *able* to survive.

But I figured it was a good idea (my own, not my Mom's). Because maybe when you get down to basics is when you find out who you really are.

P.S. And if I do find out, I'll let you know. Because *you* have *really* listened.

 188